I0687111

Also by Ev Bishop

EV BISHOP

Reeling

River's Sigh B & B, Book 6

REELING
Book 6 in the River's Sigh B & B series
Copyright © 2018 Ev Bishop

Print Edition

Published by Winding Path Books

ISBN 978-1-77265-020-4

Cover image: Kimberly Killion / The Killion Group Inc.

All rights reserved. Except for brief quotations used in critical articles or reviews, the reproduction or use of this work in whole or in part in any form, now known or hereafter invented, is forbidden without the written permission of the publisher, Winding Path Books, 1886 Creek St., Terrace, British Columbia, V8G 4Y1, Canada.

Reeling is a work of fiction. Names, characters, places, and incidents are either the product of the author's imagination or are used fictitiously, and any resemblance to actual persons, living or dead, business establishments, events or locales is entirely coincidental.

To my dad, a dear friend, a wise adviser, an occasionally silly guy—

I hate that you are gone and I miss you every day.

Thank you for your good example.

Chapter 1

THE LONG DRIVE INTO RIVER'S Sigh B & B was beautiful. Mia understood that, even while she struggled to suppress a low buzz of terror. Despite being nestled securely in her car, her heart pounded and her breath quickened. She was fenced on all sides. Thick trees cast long-armed shadows. A jungle of dark, impenetrable brush sprawled beyond the edges of the gravel road. The autumn sunshine dappled the ground with splashes of gold, but failed to brighten the formidable forest. It was like even nature was warning: anything—anyone—could hide here.

The website hadn't been exaggerating when it called River's Sigh B & B a "wilderness retreat." If she wasn't driving along an obvious road, it would be easy to believe she was in the middle of absolute nowhere. It was both horrible and perfect.

"You can do this," she muttered. "You can and you will." She caught a glimpse of her strained expression in the rearview mirror and crossed her eyes at herself. "Or you'll go crazy trying, which isn't saying much since you're practically certifiable already."

She wondered if everyone talked to themselves the way she did, but decided it didn't matter. The running conversations she held aloud were the least of her problems.

Her peppy little Mini Countryman zoomed around yet another bend, and then, all at once, she was finally *there*. A large round parking area lay empty before her, except for one old pickup that had seen better days. Here and there, barely visible through the trees and bushes, Mia caught glimpses of colorful tin. The cabins' roofs, she assumed. Another slippery eel of doubt swirled in her stomach. She'd known River's Sigh B & B was remote, but she'd envisioned the cabins being closer together, not hidden from view of the main house and from each other. Maybe she should've brought her mom or her sister with her, after all.

"Get out of the car," she commanded through gritted teeth. "You can't live like a prisoner forever."

She let out a shuddery exhale, eased her hands off her steering wheel, and tugged her plaid schoolboy cap lower around her ears—a difficult thing to do with all her hair tucked up inside it. It seemed to take her forever, but eventually she was standing outside the car, her big rolling suitcase beside her and her large rucksack over one shoulder. She clicked her key fob and heard the car's doors lock. She clicked again to be certain. Then she walked the perimeter of the vehicle and tested each door handle just to make extra sure.

Out of habit, she peered into the backseat too, knowing full well no one could be in there. She'd checked at her last gas stop and had driven nonstop since then, but what could she say? She was incapable of resisting the urge to check.

Mia had just pressed her forehead to the passenger side's window, appreciating its cold smoothness against her anxiety flushed face, when someone called her name. She practically jumped out of her skin—and banged her head on the window's rain guard. Rubbing her temple, she backed away from her car and spotted the source of the voice: a smiling woman in faded jeans and a comfy looking flannel shirt, knotted at one hip. She was close to Mia's age from the looks of it, so early thirties maybe, with a riot of long curly reddish hair. An old stiff-legged wire brush of a dog accompanied her.

"Mia!" the woman said again, but then her smile faded a little and she slowed her pace. "Mia Clark?"

"Yes, sorry, sorry. That's me, yes. I mean, hello." Mia groaned inwardly. It was like she was an imposter of herself. Even after all these years, this babbling mess she'd become was an unfamiliar stranger. And the worse part was that she was actually better now than she had been.

"I'm Jo and this is my faithful friend, Hoover." The dog gave a solemn nod in greeting, and Jo held her hand out.

Mia shook Jo's hand gingerly and cringed again,

knowing she was giving a wet fish of a handshake, but grateful she was able to touch Jo at all. It was another bit of progress, however pathetically small.

"It's nice to meet you in person, Jo. I appreciate the special arrangements you've made for me."

Jo shook her head. "It was nothing. The season slows down now anyway and—" She shook her head again.

"What?" Mia asked.

"It's just a bit surreal. You're really *you*. Your voice . . . it's Mia Clark's."

Mia was surprised by a tickle of true humor, not the put on, wise cracking kind she specialized in these days. "Well, I guess that makes sense. I *am* Mia Clark, after all."

"Yes," Jo agreed. "And I'm an idiot. Please ignore my blundering. I feel like star struck kid. I had all your albums when I was a teenager—and we're around the same age."

Bingo, Mia thought. "*Albums*, hey? Yep, we're from the same era all right."

Jo laughed, picked up Mia's massive suitcase like it weighed nothing, and started walking. "You probably hear this all the time, but you were a huge inspiration to me when I was a kid. There you were, having this crazy successful life when you'd started out with nothing just like me. You gave me the idea that maybe if a person worked hard enough . . . then, fast forward twenty years, you call to book a three month stay. I actually thought you were my sister Sam prank calling me. I almost hung up."

Mia rubbed her chin, then became aware of the pensive gesture. Aiming for casual, she stretched her arms out in front of her, like she was stiff from driving, and looked around instead. "Seems to me you have a lot. Must've worked hard."

Jo's stride didn't slow, but she followed Mia's gaze and sounded a little awestruck. "Yeah, I really do. Sometimes I have to pinch myself."

Mia remembered when she'd felt like that. Full of gratitude and mingled disbelief—that you could get paid for doing what you loved to do most in the world. It seemed like forever ago. Jo had expressed surprise that she was "really" Mia Clark, but what would shock Jo even more was the knowledge that despite Mia's claim a moment earlier, she really *wasn't* herself anymore, not in any way that counted. "You know there are wheels on that, right?"

Now Jo's step did falter. "Sorry, what?"

"My suitcase weighs a ton—but it has wheels. I feel bad about you carrying it."

Jo looked down, then waved her free hand dismissively. "I'm strong, and I don't want the gravel to wreck the rolling mechanisms."

The parking lot and the safety of Mia's vehicle were long gone now, the greenery on either side of the trail was wilder, and they still hadn't reached her cabin.

"So what's it like being famous?" Jo asked.

Mia stopped so abruptly, it was like *her* rolling mechanism suddenly broke. Her rucksack thudded painfully against her hip bone and she wished she'd put it on properly, not just slung it over her shoulder. She couldn't do this. If this was what staying here would be like, she couldn't. She just couldn't.

What if other people found out she was here? Jo seemed nice, but she was obviously a fan. And fans talked. It wasn't like Mia Clark was a big name or anything anymore, not even remotely, but even one wingnut from the past could . . .

Her heart hammered so loudly she was sure Jo could hear it. She laughed—a shrill, mirthless cackle. "I'm not famous anymore, but oh yeah, it was *totally awesome*. I mean what's cooler than being the object of other peoples' fantasies, right? And if you can collect a stalker or two? Well, that is *the best*, the absolute *best*."

Jo almost dropped Mia's suitcase and her face turned brick red, but Mia couldn't stop. "Seriously, there's nothing cooler than having people obsessed with you—some so far gone that even when you've been a nobody again for more than a decade, they still track you down, infiltrate your inner circle, your *family*, then attack you and leave you for dead because of some bizarre, imaginary betrayal."

Jo's hand flew to her mouth. "I'm so sorry—"

"No," Mia muttered abruptly, remembering her

therapist Brenda's advice to stop taking her pain out on everyone else in the world. "*I'm* sorry." The apology came with difficulty, like it was being pulled out of wet cement—which was a pretty good analogy for how she felt mood-wise these days. "You were just making small talk. You're curious. It's normal. I . . . have a tendency toward sarcasm, badly timed jokes, or weird rants when I'm anxious. I'm working on it, though— hence this ridiculous, humiliating confession."

Jo gave her a strange, contemplative look that Mia found hard to decipher, then smiled equally cryptically. "I can't wait for you to meet my sister Sam. Her husband's an author with a tight book deadline, so she'll be around lots this fall. I think you'll really click." Her smile faded a smidgeon—no doubt reading the extreme skepticism in Mia's expression. "Or you totally, totally won't."

Mia had nothing to say to that—and her lungs were trying to squeeze themselves shut with a sudden onslaught of fresh stress, so she doubted she could get a word out even if she wanted to. She stood there utterly mute, knowing she seemed horribly rude, but unable to do much about it.

When Jo realized she wasn't going to get a response, she, to her credit, continued on like they hadn't endured a big awkward pause. "I'm sorry. I didn't mean to hammer you with questions or bring up things I should've realized would be painful." Her amber eyes looked genuinely contrite, which made Mia feel extra bad. "I'll stop badgering you immediately, and please don't worry. I haven't told a soul about you coming here and I won't. As per your instructions, the only people I informed about you are my sister, my niece, my husband and that guy you and I talked about. That's it—and none of them will spill a word either."

Mia's breathing still hadn't returned to normal and her voice was still sharp with nerves. "Good, good. I mean I don't want you to think I'm some weird diva or something, and I can't imagine the press finding out about my . . . holiday, or even caring if they did, but just in case there are rumors or someone does ask about—"

"No one will say a word," Jo repeated firmly. "You want privacy and anonymity, and that's what you'll have."

They started forward again and Jo continued talking, still warmly enough, but with a less familiar, more businesslike tone. "This is Minnow cabin. If you cut through the bush, it's not far from yours, but for now we'll stick to the main trails, so you learn the layout of the place."

The tiny cabin Jo pointed to was enchanting, with cedar siding, a red tin roof and an itty-bitty sheltered porch that housed a large black rocking chair. A slab of polished wood nestled on the porch railing, forming a beautiful yet practical table. It held a pottery mug, a toddler's sippy cup, and a stack of picture books.

"My niece Aisha and her little daughter Mo live

here. Aisha's the onsite staff member I told you about. I know you want solitude, but this is a lot of it, especially for some people. It can be hard to understand what it's like until you live in it. She won't bother you, but she's nearby if you want her."

"Thank you," Mia said softly.

Jo nodded, and as they continued along the winding trail, she pointed out other cabins by name, some hidden in the bushes, some out in the open. Mia was particularly struck by a tall skinny one standing off by itself, surrounded by massive cedars. It had row upon row of windows and reminded Mia of a lighthouse. A funky wooden sign identified it as "Spring."

It felt like they'd been walking forever when the branches overhead grew denser, blocking out most of the sky, the gravel path narrowed into a soft duff trail, and the forest pressed in closer on each side. A cabin so large it was more like a full-fledged house appeared.

"Coho," Jo said, then elaborated. "It's empty right now and will probably stay that way since it sleeps eight people, and the prime fishing and holiday season is over for the year."

A mixture of relief and disappointment seeped through Mia. When she'd asked to be as far away from the main house as possible, she'd had no clue what that really meant.

Just beyond a copse of orange and yellow leafed birch trees, a little cedar cabin with a river stone chimney and a matching patio area popped into view.

Mia's flip-flopping emotions somersaulted away from trepidation and solidly back to optimism.

Jo finally stopped moving. "And *this* is Sockeye." She flourished her free hand. "Yours for as long as you want it."

Mia shook her head. "I . . . I love it."

Jo laughed. "You haven't even seen it yet, but thank you—and yes, I think you will. It's stocked with the items you requested. You should be good to go."

"Great. Thank you."

"That said, we serve breakfast in the dining hall every day between eight and ten. I know you want to keep to yourself and do your own thing, but don't hesitate to join us if you're ever in the mood. We don't need advance notice."

Mia nodded as Jo put her suitcase down and handed her a set of keys.

"And last but not least," Jo continued. "The gentleman we discussed on the phone got back to me. He's willing to give you self-defense lessons, and he's aware of what you need to conquer first."

Mia was suddenly freezing, and her palms itched and sweated. There was no doubt left in her; she'd tried to do too much too fast. Definitely. She assumed a flippant, joking air. "So the hermit will come down from his mountain? I'm impressed."

Jo raised an eyebrow. "Be careful what you wish for. He's a good guy like I said, but saying he's not a people person is the understatement of the century."

"Got it. Sounds like a gem."

Jo shuffled her feet, as if holding something back. "Okay . . ." she said eventually. "I guess that's it for me. Have a great night, enjoy your months with us, and please don't be a stranger. If you need anything, I'm here to help."

"I appreciate it, but I'm planning to make myself pretty scarce."

Jo nodded. "Just stick to the clearly marked trails on the map I e-mailed you, and follow the advice we discussed on the phone. If you do, you should be more than fine."

She turned to leave, but Mia stopped her. "And self-defense hermit guy, when is he coming by?"

"Tomorrow afternoon, one-ish, in the main dining hall."

"I'll be there."

Jo's chin bobbed again, then she lifted her hand in farewell and jogged off down the trail. She was completely out of sight in what felt like seconds. Mia set her rucksack down by the stone fire pit and pivoted in a slow circle, taking in her surroundings. Sockeye's deep purple door gleamed welcomingly, showy and dramatic against the cabin's rich cedar siding. Its jade and silver fish-shaped door knocker made her smile. The stone patio held two low-seated Adirondack chairs and a funky cast iron chiminea. She instantly pictured herself sitting out here on cool evenings, wrapped in a blanket, fire roaring away, cozily reading a book or writing in her accursed journal.

Reveling in the heady scent of pine trees, dirt and sunshine, with only the quaint cabin and ancient forest for company, Mia felt like she'd fallen back in time. She wished such a thing were actually possible. It would be lovely to rewind the clock of one's life, making damaging events and people disappear like they'd never happened.

Around her, the trees were silent, yet seemed to breathe. Mia told herself it was a comfortable solitude and almost believed it. She'd come a long way and had a lot further to go, but she'd make it. She would reclaim her independence and never make the mistake of letting anyone get close enough to fool her or hurt her again. She would regain her confidence and spontaneity—or die trying.

Didn't you already almost go that route? a nasty part of her brain quipped.

"Not funny," she snapped back.

She slipped her cell phone from her pocket. No service out here, but it still told the time: barely noon. She had hours of daylight left, and it was gorgeous and sunny—delightfully and unseasonably so, in fact. She shouldn't, and she wouldn't, waste her first day.

She grabbed a water bottle from her pack, then un-locked the purple door—which, in her head, she was starting to refer to as the purple door of possibility—and shoved her luggage inside. She shut and relocked the door without bothering to explore the cabin's interior. No doubt she'd have a night full of insomnia to do that.

Looking back the way she and Jo had come, Mia hesitated. She could retrace their steps and reinforce knowledge of terrain already covered, or—she glanced to her left, studying a thin trail that meandered off into the woods—she could kick-start this final step in her healing process with a bit of oomph. So really there wasn't a question, after all. Moving at pace she told herself was for maximum cardio benefit and not out of transparent bravado, Mia headed out on the unfamiliar trail to destinations equally unknown.

Chapter 2

JUST HIM, WOLF AND THE forest. This was right. Was how it was supposed to be now. Gray took a huge rib stretching breath, and the tightness and stress that had been riding him the past week fell away. Man, the air was good. Sweet and warm and filled with the scent of sunbaked cedar and pine. It felt more like the height of August than mid-September.

His leg was having a bad day, but even that couldn't dim his mood. He paused by a massive hemlock, braced himself with one hand on its rough bark, and bent to rub his stiff knee. It was great to be outside. No, scratch that. It was essential. True, he was not as strong as he'd once been and though it had been years since the injury, he never got used to it—or forgot his previous self. True, some days his damaged leg felt every stride like it was its first time connecting with the earth. But also true: he could still cover a fair amount of ground quickly and damaged or not, he was still stronger and fitter than a lot of guys. None of that really mattered though. The crucial factor was that the dead spot in the core of his being was less all-consuming out here. The agony of existing without Celine and Simon, though not obliterated, was eased. Sometimes he even imagined he felt life pouring into him from the trees overhead. It showed him some experiences were worth the sacrifices they called for and that some kinds of gains transcended pain.

Gray straightened up again and took another deep pull of air. For the most part, as shocking as it was, considering everything that had happened, he was content. He could handle physical pain. And the emotional side of things? Well, out here he was so removed from constant reminders that he fared pretty well in that arena too.

A crackle in the dry brush beside the trail and the sound of twigs snapping under the weight of a heavy animal killed the birdsong overhead. Gray smiled and made a soft clicking sound. Wolf crashed through a tangle of salmonberry bushes and appeared in front of Gray, tongue lolling and full of burrs. Gray rubbed his dog's broad head and scrubbed his ears. Wolf leaned in, his body weight solid and comforting against Gray's thigh, then bolted out of sight again.

Yep, this was what they both needed all right. To be back where they belonged. To be alone and free from the meddling of busybodies—hell, free from people in general with their prying questions and fury evoking sad-eyed looks of concern. It was too bad he wasn't completely self-sufficient, or he'd stop his seasonal forays into town all together. Even a few days was a few days too long.

Gray continued down the increasingly faint trail, then eased through an archway formed by two cottonwoods that had grown close together over the years. The small lake, *his lake*, as he liked to think of it, was a glinting sapphire in the golden sunlight. He skirted a stand of skinny jack pines, then froze. A rush of heat and blood ran to his face . . . and other parts.

There was a mermaid in his lake. And she was beautiful—even from just the glorious back view he had. A cascade of dark hair flowed down the creamy expanse of her bare shoulders and torso. A small waist flared into generous hips and a well-rounded—

Gray clapped a hand over his eyes. What was he? Some kind of pervert? It was like he'd never seen a naked woman before. Okay, it had been a long time, sure, but—he cut that thought off as well. He backtracked as quickly and quietly as he could, desperate to escape before she turned and saw him and thought he was a peeping Tom or something.

Familiar snuffling grunts—not at all humorous now—and a telltale crack of branches told Gray all hope of disappearing unnoticed was in vain. Wolf sprang from the bush and into the clearing, too far away for Gray to grab him. Then, in typical dog fashion, Wolf decided the complete stranger wading in the lake must desperately want to visit him. He charged down the rocky beach and across the narrow strip of sand at the water's edge.

The mermaid turned as soon as she heard Wolf—and screamed. Repeatedly. Completely undaunted, Wolf splashed through the shallows toward her.

Gray stripped off his backpack and limped-ran as fast as he could toward the shoreline. "It's all right. He's friendly. He won't hurt you."

The woman didn't appear to hear him over her increasingly loud screams. She splashed frantically at Wolf, trying to shoo him, but the dumb mutt interpreted her actions as play.

"Wolf! Down. Come." Wolf heard Gray's command and froze, but Gray could tell by the prick of his ears that the dog was deliberating whether he should listen or continue doing his own thing. It was, after all, so fun to play chase. Wolf was not the loner Gray was. Not by half, more's the pity.

"Come," Gray growled again, then repeated the clicking sound. Wolf's shoulders sagged and he heaved a deep, hard done by sigh. Finally, he turned and plowed through the water toward Gray. Lumbering up onto the beach, he dropped to his belly and grinned, tongue lolling.

The mermaid was not calmed. "What is wrong with you?" she shrieked. "That animal is a menace. I'm going to call animal control—"

Embarrassment burned through Gray. Wolf was usually a great dog, but he was a *dog*. He'd been excited, hadn't meant any harm. And who did this woman think she was anyway? Cavorting buck naked in the middle of nowhere? She was damn fortunate Wolf was a dog, not a bear or a moose—or the worst kind of animal, some less than scrupulous person.

He turned and strode away.

The woman yelled again. "That's it? You're just going to leave, no apology, no . . . nothing?"

He turned back. Damn his leg hurt. That sprint across the loose rocks on the shore had been too much.

She was crouched deeper in the water now, so her lower bits were covered, and her arms were crossed protectively over her chest. But Gray had gotten a good, if unintentional, eyeful when she'd been fending off Wolf. The image of her small firm breasts was seared in his mind. He shifted uncomfortably.

"I don't know what the hell you're doing or why you're naked in my lake, but this is private property."

"What?" She sounded genuinely shocked. Stricken even. But then something in her face tightened. "Are you calling me *naked*? That's impossible. The sales-person promised this au naturel bathing suit did not make me look nude!"

Gray floundered for something to say . . . Ah, the joke made itself clear—but how to respond did not. What kind of a whack job joked in a situation like this? He was a total stranger. For all she knew, he might be dangerous.

"No," he finally managed, like a dullard. "I said this is private land. *My* private land."

The woman wrapped her arms around herself even

tighter and huddled still lower in the water, her poor excuse for a sense of humor finally failing her. "This isn't River's Sigh B & B's property?"

And now it all made sense. This was one of Jo and Callum's city slickers. Gray sighed heavily and met the woman's eyes—just her eyes. "Nope. Mine. And I don't like company, mermaid or not."

For a second something almost like a sincere smile flashed across her face. "I'm not actually a mermaid, or not a full blood one anyway."

Gray nodded solemnly, but felt . . . what? Amused? How long had it been since he'd felt that? Maybe even longer than since the last time he'd seen someone else in less than their skivvies. "Jo and Callum's acres do edge this lake, but on the other side. You went too far."

She bit her lip and looked like she wished she could disappear.

"What are you doing anyway?" He waved his hand in her general direction. "If you were out and wanted an impromptu dip, couldn't you have, uh, left your underthings on?"

Underthings? Okay, he didn't mind being a hermit, but he didn't want to sound like some bushed weirdo either. He suspected it was too late.

Her teeth sunk even further into her bottom lip, and her eyes—bright cornflower blue, striking against her nearly black hair, though he hated that he noticed— sparkled like she was near tears. Gray felt bad. Sure, she'd surprised him, but it wasn't like she was committing a crime. Still, he didn't offer any reassurances. He didn't want to say anything that might be construed as him not minding that she was there. Because he did mind. Very much.

He turned away one last time and clicked to Wolf, who stood promptly, but threw a mournful glance over his shoulder toward the naked woman he wouldn't get to play with.

"I feel your grief, buddy," Gray whispered, shocking himself with the small joke and even grinning a little. The moment of silliness withered instantly, however. He didn't let himself entertain stupid fantasies—and thankfully they didn't pop into his head often. Which was for the best. He lived with enough chronic pain as it was.

He strode off without a backward glance, hoping like hell he wouldn't run into the skinny dipper when he was teaching self-defense lessons to the old musician Jo had begged a favor for.

Chapter 3

MIA LOCKED THE CABIN DOOR, slid the deadbolt, then slipped down to the floor. She twined her arms around her shins and pressed her chin against her denim clad knees—denim that was damp from her lake-soaked body. She'd thrown her clothes on without drying off and hightailed it back to Sockeye as fast as she could after her humiliating and terrifying run-in with the awful bushman and his savage dog.

She closed her eyes, fighting to hold herself together. It could've been worse, so much worse—but it also could have been way better. "I don't know what the hell you're doing," the man had stormed. And Mia wondered the very same thing: what *was* she doing? It was one thing to want her independent, free spirit back. It was another thing entirely to take foolish risks.

A person should be able to be free, to enjoy nature and to not be in danger, a small part of her stubbornly argued. For once Mia didn't retort out loud. She agreed with her inner self—but what *should be* and what *actually was* in this world were very different things.

All she had needed to do was follow Jo's printed

map of the grounds and she never would've found herself in that compromised position. There was even a beach on River's Sigh B & B's side of the lake, but the location of the sun and how it shone on the far shore had called to her.

Maybe all the bad things her inner-self whispered—that she deserved everything she got, that she was terrible at reading people, that she was stupid and stubborn—were true. And maybe that meant her secret, most dreaded conviction of all was true too: that if she hadn't been so bent on enjoying herself and "living life to the fullest" she would've seen Ryland for what he was and predicted his behavior. No, she insisted, forcing her thoughts to take a different track, you couldn't have. No one would've.

The stranger's scowl filled her head again. How furious her lame attempt at a joke had made him, almost like he considered her sense of humor more offensive than her trespassing. It was safe to smile about it now, so she did . . . a little.

And there, in the safety of her locked, secluded cabin, she let herself acknowledge something else. Another emotion had bubbled up when confronted by the ferocious dog and his stern master. She had been frightened, undeniably and absolutely, but she'd also been . . . curious. Still was, in fact. At first she'd thought the glowering, heavily bearded man was elderly. He sort of moved like he was. But after he'd come closer, to reprimand her more thoroughly, she'd realized he wasn't that much older than her—five or ten years, tops. His tall frame was strong and heavily-muscled, but one leg was injured or crippled or something. And, unpleasant as his presence had been for her, she'd swear he was just as uncomfortable with their encounter as she was. Maybe even more so.

It was kind of messed up to feel this way, but the idea that she could be perceived as a threat instead of as prey was shamefully refreshing.

She got to her feet slowly, ready, finally, to shed her uncomfortable, wet clothes and to explore her new home away from home. Thankfully, she'd never have to see that wild brute of a man again—a fact for which "relieved" was far too weak a word—but she had decided something important. She was going to consider her first day at River's Sigh B & B a success, lake fiasco notwithstanding. She had spent a whole afternoon alone, done something impulsive, just because she wanted to, without fanfare or a chaperone or calling anyone to check in. It had been a bit of a nightmare, sure, but she'd survived—and hadn't had a panic attack in the aftermath. She even found the incident a bit funny. It was more than she'd hoped to accomplish in weeks, let alone the first day.

Chapter 4

GRAY HAD WORKED HIMSELF INTO a small fury by the time he crossed the river and traversed the miles between its banks and Jo and Callum's establishment. He'd hardly had a wink of sleep the past night, thinking about the mermaid. That people like that, people who took their personal safety so lightly, who lived so recklessly, could dance through life untouched and thriving, while his precious Celine and little son—

His throat closed and the muscles over his sternum turned to stone, so rigid and tight he could hardly breathe. Wolf bumped one of Gray's clenched fists with his cold, wet nose and whined. Gray reached down and scratched his pet's ears. The dog, as if sensing Gray's sorrowing rage was deeper than even the norm, had been a shadow all day, never straying from the trail or letting himself get distracted by various autumn stinks. He was little comfort today, however. Gray couldn't pull himself out of the mire of his memories.

He never should've agreed to Jo's request. Never. In fact, if he hadn't been preoccupied with thoughts of winter prep—and if he wasn't feeling significantly lighter in the wallet after buying a good four months' worth of staples and arranging to have them brought up river for him in a week or two's time—he *wouldn't* have agreed to it. Not for love or money. But that was the problem, wasn't it? Both were working against him at the moment.

The problem behind his stupid decision to accept the self-defense gig was twofold. One, he liked Jo and Callum. They kept a distance he appreciated, but were good to him, even going so far as to pick up supplies for him occasionally or letting him buy goods off them directly. Plus, the odd time when nights got too long for even him, they actually seemed to enjoy a surprise visit. He wanted to be a good neighbor to them, the way they were to him.

Two, despite his simple living, he needed money. He owned his property outright, had a small disability pension, and earned extra cash with the odd small job here or there, but he wanted to go fully off-grid eventually. That would mean no income at all at some point—and would demand some expensive wish list materials. Teaching some old bird a thing or two about safety had seemed like an easy way to pad his pockets. Now Gray wasn't sure the hassle would be worth it.

Gray reached River's Sigh B & B's big dining hall without running into another soul, something he was grateful for.

"Down," he commanded as he and Wolf ascended

three stairs and crossed the deck leading to the entrance. "Stay."

Wolf sank to his belly, but his mismatched blue and brown eyes followed Gray reproachfully and seemed to say, *I thought it was dogs who barked.*

Gray didn't knock or wait for an invitation to enter, though it went against everything in his nature to intrude on someone's space without explicit permission.

"I've told you and told you," Jo had said with a laugh, pretty much every time he visited, "you have an open invitation anytime. If the dining hall's unlocked, walk in. It's a public space. No need to knock."

Yet he'd continued to knock and wait for her to come to the door—right up until three visits ago, when she finally added, cheerfully but firmly, that his insistence on being answered at the door was inconvenient for her, that she was often in the middle of putting something on the stove or pulling something from the oven. Gray apologized and from that point onward, let himself in unannounced.

Today, however, barging in didn't give him pause. He flung the big oak door open and charged inside, oblivious to whoever might be in the room. His eyes lit on Jo's smiling face and he was suddenly irrationally incensed by her warm, calm, everything's all right attitude. Things were rarely all right. The world was a cesspool. People were constantly in danger, at risk—

"You." He shrugged out of his ever-present backpack and thrust his finger at Jo, lest she somehow miss the fact that he was talking to her.

Her smile disappeared. One eyebrow arched. "Me *what*?"

"You need to do a better job controlling the imbeciles you and Callum let muck about the place. You don't own the whole river, you don't own the whole lake, and you definitely don't own the land *across* the river."

Jo's mouth fell open, but Gray was just getting started.

"You can't let your careless, numbskull tourists have free rein. It's dangerous to them and irritating to folks who have legitimate claims to these parts."

Jo had started to look cross, but now she infuriated Gray further by giggling. "*Folks who have legitimate claim to these parts*? What are you, some old black-and-white movie cowboy?"

"It's no laughing matter. You need to take my concerns seriously, or maybe I'll take them to the regional district—"

Jo's eyes narrowed and her jaw tightened, definitely cross now. Gray, even in his bizarre rage, couldn't miss it.

"I give you a lot of leeway, Gray, because of, well, everything, but you have some nerve storming in here, yelling to beat the band, not even having the manners to explain what's put a bee in your bonnet."

Yelling to beat the band? A bee in his bonnet?

Who sounded like some old movie character now? She did have a point though. He could've explained what had happened, instead going straight to shouting.

Gray pushed his hands through his hair and lowered himself into one of the chairs surrounding a huge glowing slab of cedar that formed a masterpiece of a table. His overblown reaction was probably due to adrenalin. He'd been primed and prepared to confront that disquieting nudist again and wanted to have a strong guard up. Now poor Jo had borne the brunt of his unease.

She was staring at him. He raised his hands. "I'm sorry, Jo. I had a bad night, but that's no excuse."

Her expression softened immediately—which was a prime example of why he worried about her. She was too soft, too willing to forgive. She should've tossed him out for being such a cretin. "Was it your leg?"

Her question made him realize he was unconsciously rubbing the knotted flesh and scar tissue beneath his pant leg, just above his knee.

He shrugged. "Yeah, if the old joint can be trusted for anything, I think the weather will turn soon . . . but that's not the problem." He unloaded the details—*all* the details—about the young intruder.

Jo didn't address his story immediately. Instead, she poured him a coffee from an insulated carafe. "This is left over from this morning, so it's old and cold, just how you like it."

He nodded thanks and sipped. As usual, despite her

disclaimers, it was delicious.

She refilled her own mug too and her forehead wrinkled in thought. "We don't have anyone as young as you described staying here. Until this coming weekend we only have one guest, the musician I told you about, but I don't think she has long hair."

"Why would this lake person lie about where she was staying?"

"No idea. Maybe she just wanted to avoid a hassle." Jo shrugged. "If she knows about River's Sigh B & B, she could've dropped our names, so you'd think she belonged."

"Could she be one of your sister's friends?"

Jo laughed. "No, your mysterious skinny dipper sounds a little too Bohemian for Sam's tastes."

Gray rubbed his beard. That was true. One of the things he respected about Sam was her no-nonsense approach to life. He'd seen glimpses of her softer side because she couldn't rein herself in around her romance author husband and little granddaughter Mo, or, more accurately, she didn't bother to. Gray had no doubt if Sam wanted to, she could even hide her tenderness about them. She could teach anyone a thing or two about keeping a guard up.

"Aisha's?"

"Nah. If she were Aisha's friend, Aisha and Mo would've been right there with her. Also, Aisha would never infringe on your privacy like that."

Gray didn't like even the smallest mystery. He'd

been rankled enough by the woman's presence when he thought she was linked to Jo and Callum. The idea that she was an unknown entity entirely, flitting around a place she knew nothing about, set his teeth on edge. Still, sadly, there was no cure for stupid and as much as he worried too much about too many things, she wasn't his problem.

He slurped more coffee, gladly took one of the blueberry muffins Jo offered him—and felt embarrassed when he involuntarily closed his eyes in pleasure at the first bite. He couldn't help himself though, and he'd challenge any man to be stronger. The baked treats were sweet, lemony, buttery, blueberry heaven.

"Have another," Jo urged.

Who was he to say no? He happily, or as near to happy as he ever felt in his life now, accepted one more. Then he remembered his real purpose for being there. Shoot—not just to rail about some flake in the lake and not, more's the pity, just for a social call.

He jerked his head toward the door. "So what about the old lady performing artist? She going to show up anytime soon?"

"Old lady performing artist?" Jo's forehead scrunched again.

"You know, the person you baited me into teaching self-defense?"

"Get real. I hardly *baited* you."

Gray waved his muffin and Jo's eyes twinkled.

"Okay, maybe I baited you a bit—but the woman who wants self-defense lessons isn't old . . . unless you're calling me old."

He shook his head quickly. He'd been out of the world at large long enough to become a social dimwit, but he hadn't lost his whole brain yet.

"She's right around my age."

"But I thought she was some big star back in the day."

"Yeah, but she was a teen star, like Tiffany or Debbie Gibson."

Gray knew he looked blank.

"Avril Lavigne?"

He still looked blank.

"Let me guess, you were more of a country guy in the 80s and 90s."

"Classic rock, actually."

Jo made some teasing response, but Gray hardly heard it. His brain was chugging away, making connections—and corrections—to his formerly held assumptions. If his student wasn't some sixty-plus, old-school rock star . . . if she was Jo's age.

He couldn't keep the horror out of his yelp. "But you're young!"

"Well, thanks," Jo said.

"The girl, the *woman*, in the lake . . . I said *she* was young."

Comprehension sparked in Jo's kind eyes and Gray saw amusement battle with sympathy across her features. Well, she could laugh if she wanted to. This was a disaster.

Behind Gray, the big oak door to the dining hall opened, but he had bigger things on his mind than some tourist making inquiries. "You're actually serious? You expect me to teach self-defense to a complete *idiot*?"

Jo gave a tiny, almost imperceptible shake of her head, and Gray realized his mistake immediately. She'd said they currently only had one guest staying at River's Sigh, and Gray wasn't the kind of guy who ever had any luck. That meant there was no way the person who'd entered just in time to hear him spout off was a staff member. Bristling, he turned in his chair—and his churning gut's suspicions were confirmed.

Standing motionless, her face blanched of all color, was . . . the mermaid. She was accompanied by Jo's sister Sam and was fully clothed in baggy sweatpants and an oversized navy hoody. She wore a cap pulled low over her ears, with her hair tucked up inside—but it was her, no doubt about it.

And it was absolutely no comfort that she looked as startled and unhappy to see him as he was to see her.

"I take it no introductions are needed?" Sam said wryly.

Chapter 5

MIA WAS CONSCIOUS OF THE dining room's most obvious features—a massive cedar table, floor to ceiling windows along one whole wall, a crazily amazing mountain view—but it was the nondescript door behind her, the one she'd just burst through, that held the biggest part of her attention. It wasn't too late. She could turn. She could run.

The room was fragrant with fresh coffee and baked goodies, which normally would've had her stomach growling. Right now the smell turned her stomach.

That man, that horrible jerk, from the lake in the woods was *here.* In the place that was supposed to be her sanctuary, the space she was supposed to be able to practice being by herself while knowing she was safe. How was that possible? And he was talking about self-defense classes and an idiot. Wait a minute . . . shit! He was the instructor—and she was . . . the idiot.

Beside her, Jo's blonde, model-thin sister Sam, who'd crossed Mia's path on the way to the hall and introduced herself, gave Mia a quick onceover. Then her cool green eyes fixed on the man Mia was staring at. She spoke. But what did she say? Something like "No introductions are needed?"

Hurry up, come to your senses, moron, Mia muttered to herself. She inwardly steeled her spine and outwardly chuckled. "Uh, no, we've met—sort of. He was, of all things, skinny dipping in the lake. I think my presence startled him."

"What?" The word was a roar—truly, that was the only way to describe it. The angry bushman with his overgrown beard and long curly hair leaped to his feet, looking so ferocious that Mia stepped back.

Jo's mouth fell open and she seemed at a loss for words, which Mia figured was probably unusual. Sam, however, snickered. "My, my, Gray... I never would've guessed about this secret wild side of yours. I guess you really are bushed."

Gray—at least Mia now had a name for the guy towering before her, other than "raging man"—was practically frothing. "I did not. I wasn't. It was—"

"Me, it was me." Mia threw her hands up in an exaggerated gesture of surrender. "I was just teasing him a bit."

"Lying more like it," Gray snarled.

"So now I'm a liar *and* an idiot." Mia shrugged. "I've been called worse."

"I bet you have."

"Whoa, Gray." Jo jumped to her feet to emphasize her suddenly stern tone. "I get it. We all get it. Mia startled you yesterday. I'm sure she's sorry."

"I actually am," Mia admitted.

"See, she didn't mean to make you uncomfortable."

"It is not about my discomfort," Gray roared. "It's about *safety*. Sure, in a perfect world people should be able to wander around naked or blitzed out of their minds and be safe from harm."

Mia froze as he, totally unbeknownst to him, voiced her very thoughts from the night before.

"But it's not a perfect world, is it? No, it's the furthest thing from! What if some weirdo happened across her while she was frolicking around naked as a jaybird?"

"I think that's a pretty accurate description of exactly what *did* happen." Sam arched a shapely eyebrow. "And yet here she is, perfectly well and fine."

Jo frowned at Sam, but Mia smiled with gratitude for the solidarity. Jo's observation the day before was spot on. Mia could already tell she was going to like droll, sharp-tongued Sam a lot. Gray seemed oblivious to the insult and lectured on. "There are a million places to dump a body out here where she'd never be found."

"Yikes," Sam drawled. "Should we be concerned about how you spend your time?"

Gray slumped back into the chair he'd deserted seconds earlier, and Mia was surprised when what appeared to be a flicker of hurt creased his dark brown eyes. Jo stepped close to Gray and put a hand on his shoulder. "Come on, Sam. Give him a break."

"What? I'm merely contributing to the conversation *he* initiated. He's the one acting like an expert on weirdos and spots to hide bodies."

Jo shook her head. "I'm sorry, Mia. This really is a nice, peaceful, *safe* place—and you should be able to do whatever you want on the property with no more unhappy surprises." She shot a pointed look at Gray, but he was staring down at the table and didn't notice. "I'll refresh you on the boundaries."

"I don't get it," Gray whispered, like he was talking to himself. His shoulders sagged as if all the fight had gone out of him.

Mia couldn't help but wonder what he so sadly didn't get. Then his head snapped up and his flint-like gaze—nothing kind or soft in his eyes now—locked on her once more. "I'm sorry, but I won't fit your needs as instructor. You'll have to find someone else."

"Couldn't you try one session, Gray, and see how it goes?" Jo asked. Mia was suddenly reminded of her sister Jackie. She was always trying to make peace, too.

For her part, Mia was torn. A big chunk of her wanted to defend herself, to correct the conclusions this Gray person had jumped to. She was not some risk taking, danger craving adrenaline junkie looney who only wanted self-defense lessons so she could put herself in even more outlandishly unsafe situations.

Another part wanted to tell him to take a flying leap. Where did he get off thinking he knew anything about her at all?

Dominant over every other feeling, however, was a heavy sense of futility and hopelessness. She just wanted to curl up and quit and return to her increasingly small and secluded life.

So why don't you? her mother's kind, reasonable voice asked in her head.

Because then the bastards win. You shouldn't have to stay locked in a tower to be safe, Mia replied internally—but her inner conviction wasn't as strong as it sounded.

Mia flinched suddenly, realizing she had zoned out for too long. Jo, Sam—and even Gray—were staring at her with something like concern.

She shook her head, suspecting one of them had said something that she should've responded to, but for the life of her she didn't know what. "Sorry. Come again?"

"I asked if you wanted me to see if there's someone in town who does private lessons. Some of the gyms have martial arts trainers and—"

Mia held up a hand to stop Jo's kindly intentioned barrage of words and swallowed against nausea. Some days—even a lot of days, lately—it was different, but right now the notion of going someplace, *anyplace*, in a foreign town, where there'd be so many people, so many strangers, without her mom or her sister or a hired companion made her feel physically ill. "Thank you, but no. It won't work right now."

Fully aware she was acting like the loon she'd so desperately wanted to insist to Gray that she wasn't, Mia turned on her heel and practically sprinted through the blessed door.

On the trail back to Sockeye, she imagined all the gossipy things Jo and her sister and their good friend Gray were probably saying. She didn't care. They couldn't say anything about her that she hadn't already accused herself of. The aspect of the meeting she'd choose to focus on? That she hadn't been afraid being alone with them. That was a big deal. In fact, screw "big." As small and pathetic as it might seem to some people, any occurrence of her feeling safe was huge.

Chapter 6

MIA CRACKED HER KNUCKLES AND paced Sockeye's cozy interior, but took no pleasure in its slate flooring, earthy throw rugs, and unique furniture. Even the bedding, which she had loved at first sight—gorgeous Egyptian cotton in river water hues—didn't distract her. Any time she'd wasted regarding the exploration of the cabin when she first checked in had been made up for in spades. She had every bit of the tiny place memorized right down to how many footsteps it took for her to reach the door to her bedroom from the left side of her bed and the right. She could find the front door and every window in the dark. She had reorganized the kitchen, removing the cutlery and knives from a drawer and placing their tray in a cupboard beside the fridge instead, transferring the heavy frying pan from beside the stove to under the sink. . . .

She knew, of course, that no one familiar with the layout of the cabin would be a threat to her, but as she'd already established and established and established, she slept easier if she took extra precautions. Not that she was sleeping. The first two nights had been a delight and a surprise: she'd got in a solid six or seven hours each night. Now she was back to her old wide-eyed ways.

She stopped pacing and returned to her notebook, which lay open on the cedar slab coffee table in the living room. She frowned at what she'd written.

Day 1 – Met a stranger in person (Jo) and managed to be relatively normal. Impromptu swim, interrupted/accosted by a monster of a dog and his equally monstrous owner. (You're trying to see that as a success, she reminded herself. You were spontaneous. You walked all over the place by yourself. You survived—even had fun before it went all downhill.)

Day 2 – Met another stranger (Jo's sister Sam), without warning or prior planning (extra points!) AND kept an appointment to meet with self-defense trainer. Self-defense trainer is terrible. Rethinking that plan.

Mia wanted to write a far more scathing, self-deprecating entry, describing what an idiot she'd been, but she was attempting to follow yet another bit of her therapist Brenda's advice and trying to keep a record of, and give herself kudos for, every success, no matter how minuscule. Brenda had given Mia the journal she was currently using, matter of fact, with the words "Success is just the accumulation of small goals" embossed across the front of it. So far Mia had managed to refrain from crossing the words out with black felt marker. How was that for a small goal *and* a success?

Day 3 – Stayed in.

Day 4 – Stayed in.

Day 5 –

Mia knew all too well what Day 5 would read if she wasn't careful. *Stayed in.* To an outsider, maybe it wouldn't be a big deal. To her it was . . . failure. And having this written record of her lameness? An even more epic failure.

Mia didn't have a problem, per se, with celebrating small accomplishments. She was just frustrated and exhausted by hers being *so* small. And she was missing her guitar like she'd had a limb amputated, even though she hadn't played it for months so had thought it served her right to leave it behind. And she hated this journal and its in your face positivity. Maybe she should give it up and revert to what she liked to write in—blank paged sketch books—and go back to what she liked to write—lyrics. Also, doing the latter part would be a Success. (Yes, with a capital S—but one she wouldn't write down, so there, Brenda!)

Mia could tell from her inner dialogue that she was going a bit stir crazy and it made her laugh. After all, who did it hurt if she went crazy—or crazier? She was all by herself in the woods, not a witness or a person to be affected in sight.

"I'm afraid you'll disappear into yourself again, and your sister and I won't be there to check on you and pull you back." Her mom's well-meant (and seriously irritating) concern replayed in Mia's memory. Her mom hadn't wanted her to take this trip, hadn't understood why Mia couldn't embark on some system of baby steps back into the land of the living (Mia's phrase, not her mom's. In fact, her mom hated it when she said it), while staying put with her "support system" close by. Mia had been adamant about going to the verge of rudeness. Her mom and sister, much as she appreciated and loved them, had become part of the problem. She relied on them too much.

Mia deserted the journal once more and stalked over to the living room window, spread two of the bamboo shade's slats, and scrutinized the forest beyond her cabin. What if her mother was right? Maybe she wasn't strong enough to cope on her own yet. But if not, when? It had been five years since—

She deliberately fuzzed out the details. She didn't like thinking about it directly—and didn't think it helped either. If anything, reliving the specifics time and time again felt like giving Ryland power over her—the power to keep her afraid, the power to make her constantly second guess herself.

Suffice it to say (and think!): she figured if she didn't overcome her . . . *issues* . . . soon, she most likely never would. People were creatures of habit, weren't they? And her habits were entrenched. In the same way pianists played scales until the movements were finger memory, requiring no thought, and prac-ticed guitarists changed chords unconsciously with the music, staying in, being alone, had become Mia's natural state. It was how her mind and body felt most secure, felt *right*. It was only when contemplating a need to grow, to get past this, to go out in the world that she got all angst-ridden and nutty.

Mia pulled the blind's cord, opening it fully, so though she was still separated from the outdoor world by hard, cold glass, all that she was missing was clearly displayed. The huge cedars standing guard around Sockeye's small clearing gleamed emerald in the late fall sun. The cloudless sky was a deep denim blue, like it had ripened with the season too. The path she'd explored the other day beckoned anew—but her skin itched with apprehension.

"Come on," she prodded aloud, "or day five will turn into day six, into day seven . . ."

Still unsure if she'd go through with it, she crept to the entrance way and pulled on her boots.

Once outside, Mia moved as far as the unused fire pit, then paused and evaluated her surroundings, giving her eyes a moment to adjust. Manmade light—and she'd had days of only it—was a very different animal than natural outdoor light.

She shivered. Something in the weather had changed while she'd been hiding out. It was still sunny, as she'd noted from inside the cabin, but there was a dampness beneath the heat and a chilly breeze that whispered hints of inevitable changes. The air smelled different too. It had been dry and piney when she first arrived. Now there was an earthy quality and maybe the slightest whiff of smoke, like someone was having a bonfire.

Resolutely, Mia put one foot down in front of the other and started along the trail she'd followed the other day.

It wasn't quiet. At all. Overhead, a disorganized V of Canadian geese flapped and honked, as if frustrated that they weren't getting their act together. Amber leaves crackled under her boots—yet another change in the mere days since she'd last been out. So many fallen leaves! Small animals, or she hoped they were small anyway, rustled in the dry brush on either side of her. The total absence of vehicle noise, of human noise, boomed.

"I thought that was the point," Mia huffed at herself. "You wanted to get used to being alone, doing things by yourself, unaccompanied."

It was no good, though. The bravery she'd felt her first day at River's Sigh had deserted her. She darted a glance over her shoulder, saw nothing, and forced herself to continue on.

"You don't have to go as far as you did the other day. Just down to the first creek. That'll be fine. That'll be great."

The eerie feeling of being watched was back, however—and raging out of control.

She couldn't quell the nattering stream of thought feeding her panic: not seeing someone is not the same as no one being there. Not seeing someone is not the same as no one being there. Not seeing someone is not the same as—

She wheeled around. Nothing. Nobody. Even the birds overhead had gone away.

She tried to laugh at herself, but couldn't. She could still see Sockeye cabin from where she stood. She'd gone all of what? A hundred feet?

She forced herself to walk calmly and keep her pace steady until there were only five strides to the stairs, and then, biting back a sob, she let herself run. Three steps to cross the deck. One click. One turn—

And she was safely indoors. She locked the door-knob and slid the deadbolt into place. Pressing her back against the door, she stretched her neck side to side, then forced herself to breathe in, then out, in, then out. . . .

Yes, her anxiety was definitely getting worse again. Ah well, that was the nature of the beast, right? It had seasons.

Also, as she had learned the hard way, only a fool completely ignored her gut. It was better to run when no running was needed than to tough out bad feelings and be direly mistaken.

Retrieving the landline's cordless handset just in case, Mia sidled over to the window. Standing well out of view, she opened two slats of the closed blind wide enough for her to scan the front walk and nearest edges of green space. "See? Nothing—" Her attempt at self-reassurance died on her lips.

The outside air was still. Even the small breeze had quit. Not a branch on any bush, shrub or tree moved even a leaf—except for one hedge. It trembled with movement. What the hell? There *was* someone hiding out there. Someone *was* watching her.

She closed her eyes and rubbed her forehead. This was ridiculous. It had some logical explanation. It was an animal or something. She knew it was. That didn't calm her palpitating heart, however, or dry her sweating palms.

She walked to the washroom, used it, took a long time washing her hands, then pulled her hair into a tight ponytail and washed her face too. Finally she retrieved her laptop from her bedroom and headed for the living room. Placing it on the coffee table, she hovered by the couch—then suddenly turned and sprinted for the front door. Unlocking the door in a wild, agitated frenzy, she threw it open.

"Get away from here!" she screamed in the direction of the hedge on her far left. "Leave me alone. Go home. Go!"

Nothing moved beyond the hedge and its branches were quiver-free now—but then something shifted in her peripheral vision. She swung her gaze forward and saw him. Utterly horrified, her voice died.

Chapter 7

STUNNED AND CONFUSED BY THE fury in Mia's fear-tightened features and electric blue eyes, not to mention by her shocking volume, Gray froze, one hand on the railing at the bottom of porch. Someone was obviously harassing her, but who? He surveyed the bushes and forest east of himself, the direction she had screamed in before noticing him and falling silent. He saw no one. Mia didn't seem relieved by the absence of whoever the intruder was or by his presence either. He took the stairs and crossed the porch in two bounds. "Are you all right? What's going on?"

Mia opened her mouth, but no words came out. She sagged back into the cabin, leaving the door wide open.

Gray looked around again, still saw nothing but trees and undisturbed ground, then self-consciously followed her in and lowered his backpack to the floor. If she gave even the slightest sign that she didn't want him there, he'd leave immediately—but she seemed fine with his company. Distracted, but fine. He fought to keep his voice even and calm, despite his thudding heart. "Is someone bothering you? Is someone here?"

"I . . . no." Mia shook her head, looking fragile. For a horrifying moment, Gray thought she might burst into tears. He hated tears, not because of the emotion behind them so much as because he always felt power-less to do anything to remedy them or to help.

For the first time in a long time—too long a time, he'd missed hearing her badly—Celine's voice, amused and frustrated, filled his head: Get a life, Gray. Stop trying to fix everything and everyone. It's not your job.

He recognized, as usual, the wisdom in Celine's comment, yet it was a difference between them that they'd never quite reconciled and a truth she'd always been uncomfortable with. Solving things, fixing people's problems, literally *was* his job, how he made his living—or it had been—and it was still his nature, like it or not. It wasn't as easy as she made it sound to just stop.

He heard Celine snort in response, as real as if she were standing beside him.

Then Mia, the living, breathing woman who really *was* nearby, shrugged exaggeratedly and pulled him from his chat with his dead wife. She jutted her jaw and adopted a flippant tone that grated on every one of Gray's raw nerves. "It's nothing. I got a little Blair Witch Project, that's all."

Gray didn't buy her act for a second. She'd been genuinely terror stricken, but was backpedaling now, faking she was fine. Why? He reached out to steady her, caught himself before he did, and jammed his hands, now clenched into fists, into his pockets. What was he thinking? He had no business touching her. He was already standing so close that he could smell her. Her scent, some hippy mixture of spice with a touch of oranges or something, put his senses on overdrive.

"Feeling watched?" he asked, suddenly knowing without a doubt that she was.

Mia hesitated and her eyes narrowed, like responding to him was the last thing she wanted to do. "Yeah," she finally muttered, almost angrily. "Maybe. Sort of."

Her face, which had been chalk pale beneath her tightly scraped back hair when she threw the door open in rage, turned a violent red. "I mean, whatever. It's stupid. I'm stupid. I know it was just some animal lurking around or something."

Gray did touch her now, very lightly above her elbow, wanting to comfort her. She was about to yank away when she saw, really s*aw*, his hand. Her eyes widened. He tried not to flinch as she took in his unnaturally smooth, shiny skin and studied the mottled white-pink ridge of scar tissue that snaked from beneath his plaid shirt's cuff all the way to his knuckles.

Her perusal had taken a split second at most, but it felt weighty and momentous somehow. When she lifted her gaze back to his, Gray took a large step back. "I don't know. My wife was a big proponent of intuition. She thought people, especially women, should listen to their gut . . ." He trailed off, feeling rattled. He never talked about Celine, not to anyone, and especially not to strangers. It was probably just a result of feeling her presence so strongly a minute ago. Still, it was strange. And uncomfortable. He turned away from Mia and headed back to the porch. He examined the property again, then stomped down the stairs. None of the fallen leaves gathered at the base of trees or in various hollows and crevices were disturbed or kicked around. Nothing looked amiss or out of place.

Mia remained stationary, framed by the doorway, watching him. As he started to poke around a nearby hedge, she moved slightly. He turned to look at her. She had crossed her arms over her chest and her fingers rubbed the spot his scarred hand had so briefly rested.

He trekked around the side of the house. Twigs cracked loudly under his feet, convincing him further that there was nobody else around. He would've heard them—or noted anything awry, out of habit—when he'd approached the cabin earlier.

When he returned to Mia a few minutes later and climbed the stairs to rejoin her, he shrugged silently.

She nodded, her mouth a tight white line. "There's nothing there. Like I said, I get it."

"Just because I didn't see anything doesn't mean there wasn't anything there, but I don't want you to worry either. I'm ninety-nine percent sure whatever it is, it isn't human. In fact . . . " Gray shuffled uncomfortably. "It could have been Wolf. He came across the river with me, but he's always gallivanting into the undergrowth. I thought he'd headed home alone, but maybe he was sniffing around here."

Mia looked at him, so earnest and serious-eyed that his heart throbbed a little. "That monster of yours is named Wolf? How fitting."

Gray's brow furrowed in humorous disbelief. Was she really intimidated by that big goof of a dog? Like she heard his thoughts, Mia shook her head. "No, after seeing you call him off at the lake and witnessing him lounging on the deck outside the dining hall the other day, I'm not really afraid of him—but if you don't know him, he is super intimidating." Her voice fell away, like something else had suddenly occurred to her. Gray would've paid a lot of money to know what it was.

"Anyway," she continued, after a pause where they both stood looking at each other a little awkwardly. "Thanks for checking out the bushes. And for not tearing a strip off me or making fun of me."

Gray's face warmed and he was grateful for his heavy beard. What kind of heel was he? This virtual stranger thought he'd yell at her or ridicule her when she was scared? "No thanks necessary, but why would I make fun of you?"

"Because I'm scared out here, nervous being by myself. I'm *foolhardy*. An *idiot*."

"Uh . . ." Gray's shoulders fell and his face burned hotter. "That's why I'm here actually. I hiked in to visit Jo and to come by your place here. To apologize. I was out of line. You very well may be an idiot, but I haven't known you long enough to make that judgement."

"No?"

"No." Gray wished the intensity of his desire for her to believe him would force her to do just that. "But all that aside, I would never make fun of anyone for being afraid. Bad things happen, a truth I accidentally revealed I'm obsessed with—and one I suspect you know too well. No wonder we get scared sometimes."

Mia flinched as if struck, and her face drained of color. Gray stopped speaking abruptly, hit by a surge of angst. What had he said or done now?

Chapter 8

NOTHING COULD'VE SURPRISED MIA MORE than Gray, the ferocious bushman, being kind. Kind and *understanding*. As he stood there before her on the porch, totally mute, a few things happened inside Mia's body all at once.

In her belly: a nervous twitching. What did Gray know about what she knew about bad things?

In her heart: a tight squeeze. The bad things in Gray's life—what were they? The things that left the scars she'd seen, the limp she'd witnessed?

In her mind and down her spine: an itching, crawling anger. She didn't want sympathy and she didn't want to stupidly trust a stranger, especially one who showed up on her doorstep out of nowhere, suddenly acting sympathetic and trustworthy. She'd already fallen into that trap once, thank you very much.

"What about the skinny dipping?" she blurted.

Gray turned red. Even with his heavy beard and wild hair, there was no disguising his flaming cheeks. "What about it?"

"I thought that proved I was reckless and foolish

and deserved whatever horror might befall me."

"I never said anything like that, not even close." Gray descended the stairs from the porch, gaining that much more distance from her. "And statistically, swimming in some lake in the middle of the woods is safer than a lot of other things people do without a second thought. Besides, if you have the misfortune of meeting someone whose heart is bent on doing harm, to hell with what you're wearing—or not wearing. Full body armor won't prevent them. There are no magic steps or surefire ways to stave off evil and protect ourselves."

Gray hefted the backpack he never seemed to be without and strode off. Mia stared after him. His limp was much less noticeable today, but because she'd seen it at its worst, she could still make out a slight stiffness in his gait. *Someone whose heart is bent on doing harm.* The words were old-fashioned somehow, maybe even understated in terms of talking about evil, but they struck a chord.

Gray had no way to know it, of course, but that's what had happened to her. She'd met someone whose heart was bent on harming her. And who can ever really see what lies in someone else's heart?

Gray was wrong about one thing, though. There was a way to protect yourself: never let anyone get close enough to hurt you. And really, wasn't that what he was doing living alone in the wilderness— maintaining a safe distance from whatever had hurt him? She bet it was, whether he admitted it or not. Perhaps she'd follow his lead. Not here—but somewhere else. If she could figure out a way to conquer her fear, once and for all, that is.

Chapter 9

IT HAD BEEN TWO DAYS since Gray showed up unannounced at Sockeye cabin and two days where, yet
again, the only thing Mia could write in her journal
was "Stayed in." To be fair, she could've also mentioned that she'd talked to her mom and sister, but
though chatting with them was a pleasure as always, it
felt like one more small defeat: she, as usual, sticking
to her safety zone.

It wasn't all wasted time, however. She had experienced a small epiphany—an "aha moment" as her
mom would call it. It was not enough for her to dwell
alone in the safety of a cozy B & B cabin, only talking
to her mom and sister. Yes, River's Sigh was foreign
to her, but other than that, her current day-to-day was
hardly any different than when she was ensconced in
her townhouse, only inviting her mom, sister, and
niece and nephew over as company and having anything she needed delivered.

No, if she was ever going to be able to live fully
independently again, regardless of where that was, she
needed to dramatically extend the boundaries of her

comfort zone. She had to practice running into people where she didn't expect them. She had to redevelop the ability to cope in situations where she hadn't arranged and organized every detail. She had to learn how to be comfortable with men again. And she had an idea how—the aha! If Gray could show up unannounced at her cabin door, she could bloody well return the favor.

MIA WAS SETTLED IN A deep armchair in Jo's cozy office, with Jo and Sam seated nearby. Outside the huge windows, a cloud scudded in front of the sun. The bright room darkened immediately, much the way Jo's expression just had.

"No," she said flatly, not bothering to sugarcoat her dismissal of Mia's plan. The outright rejection surprised Mia, who'd started to view Jo as a soft touch. "It's not a good idea—it's a terrible one, in fact."

Mia twinkled as hard as she could. "Oh, come on, Jo. Can an opinion like that *truly* be fact?"

Sam laughed, but Jo remained uncharmed. Apparently whatever star power Mia initially held for Jo had burned out.

Mia wrapped her hands around the mug of tea Jo had made for her. It was after one o'clock and a posted schedule near the door stated guests were on their own until seven a.m. the next day. Mia wondered if Jo regretted inviting her in and reconsidered her options in the face of Jo's refusal to help her. She had already pointed out that Gray had visited *her* uninvited and argued that a reciprocal visit would be fair, even if not exactly welcome. Jo failed to be convinced and only repeated her line about how Gray was vehemently opposed to surprises, blah, blah, blah. Maybe Mia should feign outrage, tell Jo that she'd promised to keep her location a secret, yet had told Gray the specific cabin she had booked.

No, she discarded the last idea as fast as it came. She wasn't the manipulative type and of course Jo had told Gray she was in Sockeye. He was supposed to be her self-defense teacher and meet her for lessons. It wasn't exactly Jo's fault the plan got botched. Okay, actually, it wasn't Jo's fault *at all*. Mia sighed heavily. Jo bit her lip and looked concerned.

Sam flashed her two thumbs up, which confused Mia, then stage whispered theatrically, "Yes, yes, that's it. Feign deep sorrow or disappointment. That's *exactly* how to get what you want from Jo. I couldn't do it better myself."

Mia laughed. She couldn't help it. "I'm not . . . that wasn't . . . " She shook her head. "I'm sorry, Jo. I really wasn't trying to—"

Jo rolled her eyes, quashing Mia's apology. "I know you weren't. My darling sister here sometimes forgets that normal people don't live life as one big emotional con."

Sam pouted prettily and didn't look a tad remorseful. "It's not my fault people like helping me or enjoy it when my favor shines down on them—"

Jo harrumphed.

"And you have to admit, I've gotten better."

"Maybe. Slightly. But on that related note, when is Charlie due back? You're better when you get regular—"

"Oh baby, yes." Sam waggled her eyebrows suggestively. "I'm much, *much* better when I get regular—"

"No," Jo interrupted with a groan. "Not that. *Regular reminders* to be a decent human."

"Yeah, yeah, Charlie hands those out consistently too," Sam grumbled, but her tone was affectionate. "Spoil sport."

Something in Mia panged. As much as she knew she needed to learn to live outside the safe shadow of her loyal bear-like mother and sister, she sure missed them. There was nothing more fun than being silly with people who knew you and loved you, no matter what.

Jo sipped her tea and studied Mia over the rim of her bright yellow mug. Whatever she saw made her sigh. "I'm not trying to be a jerk, Mia. I just . . . well, Gray's not the most predictable guy in the world. I want to protect you."

The feelings of warm camaraderie floating through Mia deflated and crashed.

"What?" she croaked. "What are you saying? You think he could be *dangerous*?" She could hardly make sense of it. Why would Jo suggest him for the job if he posed any risk at all? He'd been in her cabin. In her *home*. And it hadn't even fussed her too much—which had surprised her—because of Jo's endorsement. Her breathing grew rapid and uneven. Why, why, why—

Sam and Jo exchanged a look as Mia fought to slow her racing heart, then Jo rushed to explain. "Gray's not dangerous. Not at all. Not in any way." Jo stood and moved to Mia's side, then froze as if unsure what to do next, press a comforting hand to Mia's shoulder or keep away. In the end, she maintained a physical distance and Mia was glad. "I chose my words poorly. I'm sorry. By 'unpredictable' I only meant that if you caught him on a good day, he might welcome your company, but on a bad day—"

"He'll bite your head off," Sam completed Jo's sentence, then winked. "But don't worry—not literally."

Jo winced. "Yeah, what Sam said. Exactly. Callum and I have known Gray for years now, and I'm so used to him that I forgot how he comes across when you first meet him. He goes into extreme jerk mode when he's worried or anxious, especially about anything safety related, but he lightens up once he knows you a bit. I should've prepared you better. That's all I meant when I said I want to protect you—that I should've done a better job of explaining what he's like."

"Jo's right," Sam piped in again. "Gray's a weirdo, but he's a safe, helpful one."

"Are you . . . feeling a bit better?" Jo asked hesitantly, a few seconds later.

"Much. Thank you." Mia sagged in her chair. "I'm sorry. I know I'm bonkers. Things just spiral out of control really fast in my head sometimes. Believe it or not, this is me waaaaaay better than I was."

Sam set her empty mug down and stretched languidly. "I don't know why we're all so stressed about 'getting better.' It's our quirks that make us interesting."

"Maybe," Mia said, "but it's also nice if our 'quirks' don't get us stuck in some nuthouse somewhere—oh, sorry, some *rehab center*."

Sam laughed. "Point taken." She stood up and slipped her feet into impossibly cute—and impossibly tall—spiked heel ankle boots. "Anyway, I sadly have no clue as to where the hunky hermit lives, or unlike scrupulous Jo here, I'd have no qualms about telling you. I am, however, the person to take you up on the other part of your scheme. Jo's a terrible shopper, but I'm . . . well, let's just say it's my special skill set.

"Great," Jo and Mia exclaimed at the exact same time.

Jo darted a glance at Mia as if to see if she felt offended at being pawned off on Sam. "I'd love to hang out with you, but honestly, if you have your heart set on getting more comfortable in public places, Sam's your girl."

"I really appreciate it," Mia said, feeling shy. It

was a lot to ask of someone: please take me up town on shopping field trips or occasional lunch dates, but be aware I might have multiple breakdowns for no obvious reason.

"Don't thank me. You're a wish come true. Jo would be happiest if she never saw hide or hair of the real world again, but I need to go to town occasionally or I'll go insane—and then, hey, you and I will match."

Jo glared; Mia giggled; Sam carried blithely on. "Although, just so you know, referring to Greenridge as 'town' is overly generous. 'Village' is better, or hick hollow, or hobbit hamlet—"

"*Sam*," Jo said.

"What? She's going to see it for herself soon enough. Greenridge makes a peach pit look big. It's not a secret."

Jo shook her head like Sam was hopeless, which made Sam grin happily. Mia grinned too, well aware that she'd smiled and laughed more in the past half hour than she had in the previous month. She repeated her thanks for the tea and said her good-byes.

She was across the parking lot, about to start down the trail to her cabin, when Jo called, "Mia, hey. Sorry. Wait up."

Mia paused and waited with some curiosity, noticing Jo held a pen and notepad.

"I can't tell you how to get to Gray's place, just like I'll never tell anyone you're here. I have to respect his wishes for privacy. He has reasons for why he keeps to himself and I can't—"

"It's fine, Jo. Seriously." If the only reason Jo ran after her was to repeat her original apology, she was wasting her time—but then again, Mia had nothing but time, so it was all good. "I really do understand."

Jo held up the notepad. "I'm glad, but here's the thing. I realized I do have a way for you to contact him—one I don't think he'd object to or that would make him feel I'd broken any confidences."

She went on to explain that in the months that Gray didn't come out of the bush, he and Jo had a system for communicating, involving a hollow in an old tree. "It's really for in case his extended family or friends ever have an emergency and need to get in touch. They'll call me, I'll write the message and put it in the tree. Gray checks it every few days. Sometimes I leave baking. . . ."

It sounded beyond fun, like something Tom Sawyer and Huck Finn would get up to—except for the emergency part. Every few days seemed like a lot of time to elapse in case of a true problem, and what if it was Gray who had the emergency? Mia thought of how isolated she felt here, especially the first few days, and that was in a rented cabin with caretakers nearby! She shuddered a little.

Jo misread her body language. "Yeah, maybe it'd be weird."

"No, it's perfect." Mia grabbed the notepad and penned a quick message before she could chicken out.

Then she tore off the sheet, folded it in half twice and handed it to Jo. "Thank you."

Jo grinned. "It's kind of fun, hey? Like I'm Nancy Drew and he's The Recluse in the Shadowy Woods."

Mia laughed out loud. "You don't even know how close that is to exactly what I was thinking. Definitely story bookish."

Jo was halfway toward the big house when she turned once more. Mia had been watching her departure and surprised herself by yelling in a teasing voice, "Good grief, what now?"

"You know how I called Gray unpredictable?"

"Yeah?" Where was Jo headed now? She'd already explained away that comment too.

"In a more important way he's also completely *predictable*."

Mia waited.

"He'll always do the right thing. The helpful thing." Jo paused. "Even if he curses you out the whole time he does it."

Chapter 10

ALTHOUGH IT WAS STILL PLENTY warm, even in the deepest shadows, and Gray was comfortable in his shirtsleeves, there was a definite tang in the air now. The breeze carried a brisk note that the sun's heat couldn't totally camouflage, and an earthy, damp scent rose to his nostrils as he kicked along the rough trail. Fall's annual decomposition had begun, regardless of how balmy the weather was. When this teasing, prolonged summer finally ended, Gray bet the season's change would be abrupt. Wouldn't even be surprised if he went to bed after working around his place in a T-shirt one evening and woke to snow. But for now? For now the day was magnificent, not quite swimming—or skinny dipping—temperatures, but close.

That last thought made him simultaneously smile and cringe.

Wolf sprang from a rosehip covered snarl of wild rose canes and slowed to a panting walk at Gray's side.

"Nice to see you again, old sport," Gray said. "But I'd like to know where you get off to. You're gone longer and longer these days." The truth of his words made Gray pause for a second and he rubbed Wolf's thick neck. The dog was always something of a wanderer, but he really had been disappearing for unusually long stretches.

"You got a new person feeding you extra meals or something?"

Wolf just smiled and let his big pink tongue loll.

"Fine, don't tell me."

Wolf grinned even more broadly.

Ahead of them, the path opened up. First, the tree cover grew sparse. Then there were no trees at all, just a wide expanse of loose round stones as they neared the river. The bank still showed telltale signs of the heavy skid of goods Gray had winched up from the rocky beach and hidden in the bush. Then, over the course of the past week, he'd transported item by item to his homestead, with the help of his trusty wheelbarrow. Right now the path he'd forged—going the opposite way he'd just come—was obvious, but over the next few days, the long grasses, small saplings and shrubs would spring back and make his trail invisible again to all but the most practiced eye. Out of habit he glanced toward the tree he kept his winch rigged to all year long. Even looking for it, it was difficult to spot.

He nodded with satisfaction then rolled his pants above his knees and peeled off his boots and socks. Stepping gingerly because he didn't go barefoot very often—couldn't risk cutting his foot or getting a bad sliver—he waded into the shallowest part of the river.

The icy water stabbed like knives at his poor feet and calves, but he only had another month at most to take advantage of reaching the Secret Keeper—Jo's name for their tree, which he had to admit he found very fun—by this route. The majority of the year, the river was too treacherous to cross and he'd have to take the long way, down and around to the much smaller creek with its makeshift bridge.

When Gray got to the Secret Keeper and reached into it, he smiled. He had mail! There was a time when that might have caused anxiety—the tree was supposed to be for emergencies, after all—but in the years since he'd gotten to know Jo, it had become a source of treats and the odd invitation. Now if it ever bore bad news, Gray figured he'd have to reread the note ten times to get it through his thick skull that it wasn't an "enjoy these new dessert bars" kind of message.

And that was how he felt right now, rereading the letter for a third time—that it would take another seven reads to confirm what he was seeing.

Dear Gray,

I hope you'll forgive my intrusion on your privacy, but I would like to see you. Jo volunteered to deliver this note and said she'll give me your reply. (If any.)

Thank you,
Mia

I would like to see you. The words repeated in Gray's head even after he had refolded the note and shoved it into his jeans' pocket. What did she mean by that? He knew enough from listening to Jo and Sam that "seeing" a person was another term for dating, but surely . . . no. That wasn't what Mia meant. It couldn't be. She could barely stand making eye contact with him. Also, he was a confirmed hermit. Ask anyone. And hermits don't date—er, *see*—people. Shit. It was like he was trying to convince *himself.*

Gray withdrew the note from his pocket, unfolded it again, and reread it once more, though he already had it locked away cold, word for word, in his memory. She probably just wanted to see if he'd changed his mind about self-defense lessons. And maybe he had. He'd thought a lot about her tight, fearful expression and her out of control raging panic.

Heart pounding like a jackhammer, Gray reached into his pack and grabbed the waterproof marker he always carried. Then, before he could change his mind, he filled the back of Mia's note with a black scrawl:

M,

Get Jo to tell you how to find my place and come any day this week after noon.

G

TWO DAYS PASSED, THEN THREE. Gray spent a lot of time chopping wood and pulling out the last of his vegetables—except for his cabbages that liked a hard frost before being harvested—and finally decided that Mia had changed her mind about "seeing" him.

You're not disappointed, he lectured himself. You're irritated that she bothered you in the first place.

Yeah, right. Even with his finely-honed self-delusion tools, he didn't buy his own line. But why was he so distracted by the notion she might come by? Why was he so eager for a visit? Because he'd been seeing too much of people lately as it was, that's why. He was getting soft.

Gray stepped back from his woodpile and wiped his sweating brow with his forearm, just as Celine spoke soft and clear near his ear. "You're lonely," she said point-blank.

Gray jumped and a shiver ran down his back. Then he gritted his teeth. "No effin shit, Celine!"

Auditory hallucinations. That's what one of the many shrinks he'd seen after the bombing that stole his family called these once common, now rarer, visits from his deceased wife, but Gray had never been sure that's all they were. Even now the hair tickled on the back of his neck, exactly the way one's did when warm breath, close by, touched skin. During his appointments, he'd still thought he might want to return to the job one day, so he'd been loath to share that he not only heard Celine and Simon, he saw them too. They popped by in the late hours of evening, woke him with chatter in the morning, or darted away in parking lots, hurrying to do whatever errands the afterlife called them to.

"A perfectly normal phase in the grieving process," the same shrink had reassured. But Gray was skeptical. He knew full well the lies a person told themselves to keep madness at bay, to explain the unexplainable, to try to rationalize the irrational. There were countless events and phenomena that humans couldn't satisfactorily answer for, yet the world continued to turn and in order to survive, people continued to strive to make sense of the things that befell them.

In the end, Gray decided for himself that Celine's and Simon's drop-ins were figments of his imagination, if only because of the language he used with her now—like effin shit, for example. She never would've stood for that back in the day. But even in this, it was possible he was fooling himself. Celine's death could've changed her; it certainly had him.

Her voice came again. "Maybe—"

"No!" The word exploded out of Gray. Whatever Celine was going to say—he knew the gist—he didn't want to hear it. He'd heard it all from her before.

"Well, someone's in a mood," she teased lightly.

"No," he croaked. "Don't joke. I can't. You. Our little boy. That's all I'm strong enough to love. To lose."

"Oh, hon . . . " Celine's voice was heavy with sorrow, and Gray felt the weight of her hand rest fleeting-ly on his shoulder, then drift off.

After a long minute, Gray wearily removed his sweat-soaked shirt. In a wretched way, he was glad Celine had stopped in. The stretches between her visits were longer and longer nowadays, and during all their reassurances, there was something none of the shrinks bothered to tell him. That as much as visits from his dearly departed made him think he'd lost his marbles, he'd miss the torturous moments with a physical ache when they stopped.

Gray stretched his shoulders and neck, forced his head back on straight, then lay his shirt over a hardy lavender bush. He had a small clothesline rigged up behind the cabin, but the lavender would scent the fabric nicely and the sun was hotter on this side of the house. It still amazed him how effective sunlight was at cleaning clothes. Well, maybe not for greasy items, but for clean sweat? Absolutely. The shirt would be fresh as a daisy—or as a lavender plant—in no time.

Returning to his chopping block, he grabbed his splitting maul and axe and stashed them in the corner of his packed woodshed. The wood he was doing now was all gravy. He'd had what he'd use this winter readied over two months ago.

He intentionally avoided looking in the direction of either of the trails that led to his place. It was pointless. Mia probably didn't want to traipse through unfamiliar forest to find him. He'd thought about that gaff too late, after he'd already placed his reply in the tree and hoofed it home. Oh well, it was probably for the best anyway.

He headed into the cabin and dumped water he had sitting on his cast iron cook stove into his metal washtub—and repeated the mental reminder. It really was for the best that she didn't come by, that they didn't kindle some type of, *any type of*, relationship.

He removed his pendant, bent low over the tub and scrubbed his hair and beard, then used a cloth on his face, chest and armpits. Next he lathered up with a bar of homemade soap Jo had given him. There really was no end to the things she and Callum concocted in their kitchen. Why did that thought make his gut hollow? Because he used to have someone he never got tired of being with too, someone who enjoyed making a home with him—and *for* him and their son. And because, try as he might to ignore it, these days the pain of his loss was almost matched by the pain of . . . longing. He rinsed off vigorously, trying to ignore the flood of fury caused by admitting he was lonely, even to himself. This was all Mia's fault. Until he'd met her—and felt unwanted attraction to her—he'd been able to keep a tight lid on all unrealistic thoughts and desires.

He'd just toweled off and slipped his pendant back over his head when he heard a shuffling noise outside. He'd been living in the wilds for so long, and it was the right time of year, that his first thought was bear. He snatched up his big antique cowbell, grabbed his rifle from by the door, and charged outside, dressed only in his jeans and boots. Clanging the loud metal bell in one hand, waving his rifle in the other, he hollered at the top of his lungs, "Go on now, get out of here, shoo. Shoo!"

He practically bulldozed right over Mia.

"What?" It was more a yelp of sound than an articulated word and Gray stopped in his tracks, rifle midair, bell still ringing though he'd stopped shaking it.

"Uh," he said. "You're not a bear."

"Nope, I'm not—but nice apology."

"I wasn't apologizing. I was explaining. I thought you were a bear. You're not." Gray shook his head at his own stupidity. Mia. Here. At his cabin in the middle of woods. It didn't matter that he'd invited her, or that he'd thought about pretty much nothing else over the last seventy-two hours, other than *what if* she actually showed up. He was still shocked to see her. Couldn't have been more shocked, in fact.

"You startled me. I wasn't expecting you."

"Yes, we really have to stop meeting like this."

For a second, Gray didn't understand what she meant. Then he got it. She'd greeted him the same way the other day, yelling and shooing some imaginary beast when he showed up unannounced. It was pretty funny—but the idea that he found it so made him speechless.

Mia rocked back and forth on the heels of her hiking boots and scanned his cabin, the nearby woodshed, his big old chopping block, and the garden area that was pretty much cleaned out and waiting for winter now. She looked uncomfortable and awkward, but also unapologetically curious. "I thought you'd be expecting me. It's still this week and it's past noon."

He nodded like a dullard. He'd only ever had Jo and Callum visit and not very often at that. Plus, they'd stayed in the yard, never entered the cabin because it was under construction. Or that was the excuse he'd made as he brought them coffee outside. Mia wasn't going to want to come inside, was she? What had he been thinking?

It did not get less awkward—at least not for him. He showed her around like he was a realtor at an open house, needlessly explaining each feature of his home, from the solar panels he used to provide a few hours of electricity each night, to the pulley-and-bucket system he'd rigged to draw water from the creek, to the reasoning behind where his outhouse was placed and why it bore a small sign that read, "Take time to smell the lilacs." (Because lilac bushes were traditionally planted by old homestead privies to help mask the odor.)

He managed not to grin like an idiot when she chuckled at his explanation, but did a poorer job of hiding his pride when she oohed and ahhed over his cleaned out garden. It was pretty, though. The nasturtiums were still brilliant and prolific, and somehow the freshly turned soil, all ready for winter, looked full of possibility, not like a foreshadower of death.

She studied the food he had stored in the root cellar he'd dug into a hill behind the cabin like she was taking notes.

By the time they'd finished the tour, Gray was sweating like he'd run from town and back. Mia hovered expectantly by his cabin's door, but Gray shook his head. "I don't think, I mean, I'm not sure . . . "

Mia backed away from the stoop as if burned. "Oh, of course. I get it."

What did she "get" exactly? That he was a darned fool? Why was he being so strange? She'd wanted to see him, presumably to discuss personal safety techniques, and he, whether he liked it or not, had invited her to come. After getting her to hike all this way, then forcing her to endure his weird homesteading 101 lectures, it would be bizarre to turn her away without so much as a cup of tea.

He sighed heavily, shook his head again, then pushed his hand through his damp hair. "That is to say, if you want to come in, I could make you tea."

Gray gripped the doorknob as he waited for her response—but now she was the one who seemed to have reservations. Her blue eyes darkened, and she chewed her bottom lip. Finally, she gave a firm nod. "Okay, yes. That would be nice. Thank you."

Wanting absolutely nothing more than to rescind

the offer and send Mia back to where she'd come from, Gray opened his door and ushered her into the shelter of his sturdily constructed walls.

Chapter 11

MIA COULD HAVE BREATHED IN the scent of the snug little cabin all day. It smelled delicious and unexpectedly domesticated and homey, not wild or scary at all: notes of lavender, masculine deodorant, and vanilla, like maybe Gray had been baking.

Everywhere Mia looked, something of interest caught her eye—something she wanted to touch. A flannel and denim patchwork quilt on an ancient looking rocking chair. Rocks and bits of broken ceramic and green glass lining the window's sill. The spines of surprisingly current novels arranged neatly in a tall narrow bookcase. An oddly out of place action figure with a homemade cape. A child-sized pair of rubber boots made to look like frogs, complete with bulging eyes on the tip of each boot's toe. . . .

Although the cabin was warm, a frisson of awareness made her shiver. Her desire to touch things extended to Gray. She wanted to touch *Gray*. To run her hands over his impossibly defined chest and abs. The majority of his skin was a warm honey brown that spoke, as did his muscles, of heavy physical work done bareback under the wide-open sky. He had deep scarring along his left side, however, similar to what she'd first observed on his wrist and hand. It didn't mar the beauty of his body. If anything, the damage made her feel a strange kinship with Gray and her insides panged with empathetic recognition. How badly, *how deeply*, you could be hurt and still survive.

And maybe part of her was slightly envious. If you bore physical proof of your wounds, if people could see your scars, did it make them less judgmental? Celebrity-centered "news" passes quickly and she rarely heard of her name or her case being mentioned online or anywhere else these days, but she'd never forget the hateful backlash *against her* from complete strangers, castigating her, blaming her, suggesting she was nothing more than a desperate, washed up star going for a publicity grab, when some hack got wind that Mia Clark, the child star from way back when, had a stalker issue.

Gray shifted his weight and her attention zipped back to him full-force—a welcome, if embarrassing, diversion from the old familiar circular thoughts.

She actively refrained from ogling him, but felt like she was wearing a sign around her neck that announced, "I find you ridiculously attractive and that's why I'm not looking at you at all." Somehow carefully *not* studying him seemed more telling than if she'd feasted her eyes. Her face—her entire body, actually—flamed.

How, how, *how* had she not known, not realized that the whole reason she'd wanted to see Gray again was not because she was so committed to her self-help plan, but was, instead, the product of what? Curiosity? Desire? Animal magnetism? All three? Bing, bing, bing—we have a winner. She supposed she should consider her raging attraction to Gray another "success" and let herself off the hook. It had been so long since she felt anything except dead in terms of sexual desire that she thought Ryland had killed off that part of her forever. But now . . . here . . . well, ah . . . *awkward*.

She inched toward the back wall, hyperconscious of every one of Gray's movements as he filled a cast iron kettle from a pitcher stored on a rough-hewn shelf and placed it on the adorable wood cook stove, then rustled around building a fire in the stove's belly. And speaking of fires in one's belly. She fought hard to keep her focus away from the neatly made bed in the corner, with its soft plaid comforter and plentiful pillows. Instead, she fixed her gaze on, of all things, a cherry red Gibson J-45. Gray must be a serious musician. The gorgeous vintage guitar held a position of prominence on the light pine wall. Great. She'd zeroed in on the only other thing in the room guaranteed to exacerbate her pathetic longings.

She pulled her cap off and her hair tumbled down her back in a big mess, but she didn't care. She felt like she might spontaneously burst into flames of humiliation and thwarted desire. Fanning her face with her hat, trying—and failing, she was sure—to act like being too hot was normal for her, she struggled for something to say.

At the door, before Gray offered her tea, it had been crystal clear that the last thing he wanted to do was invite her in. Why hadn't she taken the hint, said her piece (that she now realized was totally deluded!) and made tracks? Why had she thought it would be good to push herself one step further out of her comfort zone? She hadn't even known the zone she was actually in! Was she ever going to know herself or be able to trust her own judgement again?

"I'm sorry," Gray said suddenly, his voice a self-conscious growl behind her. "I know it's warm in here, maybe even stuffy. My joints like heat."

Somehow it made her feel better that he sounded as disconcerted as she felt. She decided to be honest—or as honest as she could be without making him write her off as a wing nut for sure. She felt safe around him and he was a very... manly... man. (Ugh, she embarrassed herself thinking such stupid, girly things, even in the privacy of her own head!) Still, it made logical sense that she, doing so much better these days and feeling comfortable, would experience attraction. Gray didn't have to know about it, and now that she recognized the problem, she'd deal with it and end the feelings appropriately. There was no reason he couldn't still help her.

"Your home is lovely, and the temperature is fine. I'm just not used to being in confined spaces with people I don't know well." She turned slightly—and found him studying her as intently as she had been wanting to study him. Her body temperature spiked again.

"People?" he asked. "Or men?"

She shrugged one shoulder but managed to maintain eye contact. "Pretty much all, but yes, males are . . . worse."

That's not even a lie, she reassured herself. You do find it more difficult to control your anxiety around men than women. He doesn't need to know the humiliating layer adding to your current dysfunction.

Gray laced his fingers together, then stretched his arms, palms out. His knuckles cracked, but it was the ripple of movement in his pecs that really caught her off guard. Lord have mercy. She zipped her attention back to the guitar. "Do you play?"

Gray stepped closer. Why?

He reached out and took the guitar down. Oh . . . Mia tried not to be disappointed. What was wrong with her?

"Badly," he said.

"What?"

"You asked if I play. I answered. Badly." Gray eased away again, taking the guitar with him. He moved to his small kitchen table, plunked down on one of the two dining chairs, and propped the guitar on his knee.

While his guitar posture was decent—and having justifiable reason to gawk at him was very appreciated—listening to him bang out a few chords was torture. Mia had assumed he was being modest when he said he played badly, but really it was an understatement. He was terrible, and the poor instrument was so out of tune it was a travesty. When he started murdering the main riff for Deep Purple's "Smoke on the Water"—something Mia hadn't thought possible—she grabbed the guitar from him.

"That's too nice an instrument for you to make sound that bad."

Gray's eyes twinkled with wry humor and he ducked his head in shy agreement. "I might've heard something like that before."

Mia felt herself smiling back and her stomach lurched. In this rustic, glorious place, with his golden-brown mane curling lightly as it dried and his tanned muscles glistening in the afternoon sun streaming through the window, Gray looked like some half-tamed forest god.

She settled on the edge of the other chair and began tuning the instrument. When what she was doing—handling a guitar with pleasure, not anxiety—sank in, she paused, but only for a second. When the Gibson sounded pretty good, she strummed a few times. Then, singing along, so softly the words were barely breath, she fingerpicked Bill Withers' "Ain't no sunshine." It was the song she'd played last and one that was symbolic for her.

Gray's head bowed, and he clasp the melted chunk of gold he wore around his neck as she sang.

The cabin was set in a deeply silent place. Mia had been conscious of the quiet the whole time she'd searched for it. When they'd been outside together, the fits and starts of her and Gray's disjointed conversation had been like bird chatter—a brief noise scattered over silence that existed beneath sound, completely unbroken. Now, with her song finished and Gray still as a statue, it was beyond quiet. Her singing had done something, but she didn't know what.

A bubbling hiss from the stove made her jump. Gray loosened his grip on the lumpy pendant and it fell back to its resting place above his heart. "Tea water's ready," he said, getting to his feet. He grabbed a long-sleeved flannel shirt, pushed his arms into it, did up a few buttons, then moved to the stove.

Mia watched him plop two teabags into a Brown Betty, which he filled from the steaming kettle. He put two mugs on the table, along with a tin of sugar cubes and a small can of evaporated milk. Using a jackknife, he punctured the top of the can on two sides and widened one of the openings to form a spout.

When the tea had steeped about five minutes, he poured her a mug and watched her doctor it. Then he filled his own and added canned milk. "It was my wife Celine's guitar," he said in a tone that suggested she'd asked—and asked rudely at that. "And the song you played was very apt."

If it was so "apt," why did he sound so furious? It was on the tip of Mia's tongue to respond snippily, to say that the least he could do if he was going to take his wife's guitar in some divorce settlement was to keep it tuned and in good shape. But then the significance of him having the guitar at all—wouldn't a personal item like that stay with its owner?—the misshapen chunk of gold he wore around his neck, and the action figure toy struck her all at once. Gray wasn't divorced; he was *widowed*. His wife had died somehow and maybe a child, too. Was that how he'd gotten his physical scars as well? Had they all been in some accident or something?

On the heels of that realization, Gray's choice to live alone, roughing it in the wilderness, no longer seemed brave and enviable. Mia sympathized with him—but also felt bitter. How typical. She would gravitate toward a person as damaged as she was and mistake him for someone who might be able to help her learn how to survive and thrive again. Likewise, her wish to emulate him, to cloister herself away, seemed foolish now. Yes, the cozy, isolated cottage offered protection of a sort, but at what cost?

"Healing" herself to arrive at a point where she could be like Gray and need no one, *see* no one for months at a stretch, wouldn't be healing at all. It would be regression. She'd been on the right track when she

first arrived. She needed to be able to form relation-
ships, enjoy people, trust again. . . .

Mia picked up her mug and sipped the strong,
milky tea. It was good.

After a lengthy spell, she broke the quiet. "I'm sorry if you felt the song was directed at you. It wasn't. It
was about me. Something, someone, I lost." *Myself*—
she thought, but didn't say.

Gray shrugged and downed the last of his tea.

"But that brings me to why I wanted to see you. I
miss the sunshine. I want it back."

"And you think *I* can help with that?"

Mia glanced around the cabin. Its atmosphere had
changed, still beautiful, but haunted now. The isolated
cell of a mourning monk, complete with revered, holy
articles. She nodded slowly. "I had thought so . . . or
had hoped, anyway."

"Since you're so fond of old tunes, you're no doubt
familiar with the Stones' 'You Can't Always Get What
You Want'?"

Mia nodded. "Of course." She smiled—a bit tense-
ly, true, but still a smile. "I'm especially kick ass at the
part about how if you try, sometimes you find what
you need."

Gray crossed his arms over his now fully covered
chest, but the tightness in his eyes eased a tad. "Point
taken."

"So you'll help?"

"I guess I can teach you a few things, but you'd

better tell me what you hope to achieve. I'm no magic worker."

That was fair, so Mia filled him in with the barest details. "I've been out of the music business, well, the performing side of it anyway, for years—like we're talking almost two decades—but every once in a while I still get fan mail, or someone tracks down my personal details through social media and makes contact. Mostly it's nice stuff, sort of like what Jo expresses, how I inspired them when they were young, blah, blah, blah." Mia was horrified to feel tears at the back of her throat, so she barked a laugh. "It's hard on the ego, you know? Nothing makes you feel your age more than middle-aged folks talking about your teeny bopper career."

Gray shook his head and didn't appear fooled by her attempt at casual levity. "You said you left the performing side of the industry years back. What part are you still involved with?"

Mia blushed. All these years later and she still felt a bit like a spoiled twit. "Truth is, I haven't had to work, though I've chosen to. My mom was my manager—but not a shifty, shady one like you sometimes hear kid stars get stuck with. She arranged, with my permission, for me to live off a fairly modest allowance and she invested the rest—wisely. I didn't get to spend like a Hollywood diva and the result is that my six-year career is still yielding returns that take care of me."

"Wow," said Gray.

He sounded sincere not critical, and Mia nodded. "So anyway, like I said, despite not strictly needing to, I do work—or I did. I have a music studio and before the total shit storm that almost destroyed everything, I taught guitar, voice, and song writing. And I still have an agent who sells songs I write to other people who produce them—not that I've put out very many the past few years."

Gray nodded, but his furrowed brow suggested she was talking about an alien world. "You said you mostly get nice fan mail and contact. What's the not so nice stuff?"

"Ah, you know." Mia refilled her mug from the teapot—then Gray's too. She couldn't believe she was openly talking about this. Her stupid journal would get a page full tonight.

"I can imagine, maybe, but no, I don't really know." Gray added a generous portion of the canned milk to both their cups.

"The odd creep making pervy comments, the occasional marriage proposal—"

Gray choked on his mouthful of fresh tea. "Seriously?"

Mia couldn't bring herself to laugh. Some people found it funny and maybe on one level it was, but there was also something awful and skin-crawlingly sickening beneath the idea that her whole life—even when she'd been a young, young teenager—there'd been older men lusting after her, and that even now, people looked up her old videos and felt they knew her or had some connection to her.

Gray wasn't amused either. "Disgusting," he muttered, then gestured for her to continue. The harsh word didn't seem targeted at her though. It sounded sympathetic, like he got why it bothered her.

"My mom hadn't been prepared for all that. I guess if you're not a sicko yourself, you don't always see what the dangers will be—but she took every case seriously. I feel badly for public figures today. They have it way worse. The Internet was in its infancy at the height of my career. That protected me a lot, but I still had bodyguards whenever I made appearances in public into my early twenties. After I 'officially' retired, it didn't seem necessary . . . and while the odd letter, again, mostly good, still came, I got laxer. I admit it."

Mia sipped her tea again. "I just wanted to be a normal woman, work at what I loved . . . maybe meet someone and fall in love. My dating life was . . . stunted, to say the least."

If there was something her mother hadn't done right, it was how she'd handled Mia's social life—or rather, her absolute lack of one. She hadn't trusted the "Hollywood types" in Mia's performing circle and had always put off her desire to date and have friends as something she could do later. Mia didn't blame her—anymore—but she did wonder if she'd have done a better job at spotting Ryland's true nature if she'd had more experience with men.

"Have you always had anxiety issues, or are they part of the PTSD caused by the 'shit storm' you referred to?"

Mia almost asked how he knew she had anxiety, but bit the question back. It was pretty obvious how he'd figured it out. If Jo hadn't told him when arranging the self-defense lessons on Mia's behalf, her blind-with-panic, screaming at inanimate objects, completely oblivious to his presence freak out on the porch the other day would've cued him.

"The shit storm . . . yeah." She swallowed hard, then relayed how she'd received a nasty letter one day, close to five years ago, but hadn't thought much about it—until she'd gotten three or four in unusually close succession and realized that they sounded like they came from the same person. Around the same time, she also started getting harassing phone calls, always from untraceable numbers or public phones in other cities, nowhere near where she lived.

"Other things in my life were going well, though. My teaching was very satisfying. I was playing with a band for fun . . . I'd started dating a bit—guys who were interested in me, not in Mia Clark. I figured if I ignored the new haters, sticks and stones and all that, eventually the person or persons responsible would get bored or find a new obsession and move on."

Gray made an angry huffing sound and got up and

strode to a cupboard. "I'm having bread and jam. Want some?"

"Uh, sure . . ."

He returned a second later with a loaf of uncut homemade bread, a foil wrapped block of butter, and a canning jar with a white sticker labelled "Rasp." in black marker.

"You make your own bread and jam?"

Gray shrugged and sliced two fat wedges of the fragrant loaf. "I do a lot of things. I have a lot of time on my hands."

Despite her tension, Mia laughed. She *so* related. When she was having her inside-only days back at home, she got tons done and had never had such an immaculate house. She buttered her bread and added a generous scoop of jam. "Mmm," she said, a little surprised when she took her first bite. "This is amazing."

"Thanks." Gray ate his piece in three gulps, like he was doing it for sustenance, not enjoyment. Mia took one more bite, then put the rest down for later.

"And then I met someone different. Someone potentially serious." The words sounded so innocuous, so normal . . . so the opposite of absolutely everything that followed.

Gray nodded.

"And he, it, our relationship, was wonderful. Until it wasn't. Until it turned out he was behind the increasingly hideous and threatening letters and calls—and was feeling more and more frustrated by how they didn't seem to be getting to me. Until he had moved into my home, had access to my computer and finances, was part of my business and family life—" Mia spoke in rush, racing to get the details she needed to share with Gray out before they caught up with her emotions, desperate to not relive them in any way in front of him. Her hope was in vain.

It was like she could feel Ryland's hand close on her shoulder. She shoved at it—but, of course, nothing was there. Except . . . was that his breath prickling the hairs on her neck? His cologne clogging her senses? Could she *smell* him? And when she'd smelled him *then*, had her heart pulsed a little at the scent, had a bit of happiness tingled through her at his touch before she realized—

She gagged lightly, set her mug down. "He . . ." She flapped her hands. Where were the damn words? Where?

"Mia," Gray said softly, then again, more insistently, *"Mia."*

"What?"

"You can tell me anything you need to, but don't feel you have to unless you want to. I know what it's like to be gutted. I understand. He hurt you. He was someone you trusted, were intimate with and he hurt you."

"Yes." It was enough. She had never found words to capture the physical terror—of how it was like feeling each of her body's systems shutting down. She couldn't articulate the grief and shock and hatred that coursed through her when her own body betrayed her, priming for pleasure while her mind struggled against the knowledge she was about to be raped. Could still barely reconcile this new version of herself with the person who endured things no one should have to—all while fighting just to live, just not to die—at the hands of a man she had thought loved her.

That had been the most terrifying, mind sickening, soul destroying part of all: that she was trying to survive *Ryland.* Someone she knew, that she'd let into her heart, that she loved, was a monster. Was trying to kill her. *Had wanted to do her harm for a long time.*

Mia's pulse jumped at her throat and her heart thudded painfully in her chest. "I should've seen him for what he was, right?"

Gray shook his head. "How? It's like you said about your mom. If you're not a sicko—I'd call it evil—you don't always see what the dangers are. Can't even."

"But I dismissed all those letters, all those increasingly threatening warnings. I invited him in. I gave him every opportunity . . . It wasn't entirely, but maybe it was partially my—"

"No, it wasn't. Not in any way. Period." Gray's tone allowed for no argument and for a moment, even the most insidious voices ever present in her psyche were temporarily silenced.

She picked up her snack again but couldn't take a bite. Her mouth was dry, her throat too tight to swallow. She managed to take a breath, then another. Then a sip of her cooled tea.

Gray sat quietly, at ease, like their conversation and now their silence was exactly right and normal. Finally, she could speak again. "So that's why I'm here. I have come a huge way since . . . all that. For a long time, I literally couldn't leave my condo. Then I couldn't leave without my mom or my sister. I am . . . better. But I still have really intensely bad moments where the fear that someone I trust or a danger I don't pick up on right away will hurt me. I . . . I can't bear even the lightest, most casual touches—though I don't scream, now at least, if someone touches me accidentally. I thought that having even a rudimentary knowledge of how to defend myself physically, might help me handle social or public gatherings more confidently."

Gray picked up his tea and drank it down, studying her. "We can meet three times a week, if that works for you, and I'll give you a workout schedule to follow."

Mia nodded.

"You won't like my top two pieces of advice for self-protection though."

She waited.

"One, don't let yourself get in a dangerous spot in the first place."

A choked sound escaped Mia, and Gray held up his

hand, "If you can help it, and that's a big *if*. Like we discussed earlier, sometimes there's no way to predict trouble or to avoid it. We still have to live." As those last words fell from his mouth, an expression Mia couldn't interpret twisted Gray's features. She nodded hesitantly.

"Two," he continued more ferociously than before, "if you do find yourself in an unsafe situation, or even just an unknown one, get out of there. Leave. Run—as fast and as far as you can. Putting distance between yourself and whatever is threatening you is always your best chance of protection."

She nodded again, unable to avoid a sense of throbbing shame even though she knew intellectually she wasn't to blame for what happened or for not stopping it—and that Gray wasn't saying she was.

"One more thing," Gray said softly. "I don't know if it will help you, but it helps me . . . some things that happen are so terrible that no matter how shitty, random, and cruel life sometimes is, the chance of them reoccurring is minuscule."

"Gee, thanks, that's super comforting." Strangely, though, she did feel better.

Gray shrugged. "You're the one who came to me. I'm sure people recommended against it."

"They did, actually," Mia admitted. Then she laughed—and it was a sincere, mirth-fueled *laugh*. How had she gone from what she had been feeling to this light-hearted, comfortable . . . mirth? Gray shook his head.

"We're a great pair, hey?" she said.

"No," Gray said. "We're not. Now are you going to eat the rest of your bread or what?"

Chapter 12

THE LEAVES CRUNCHING UNDER GRAY'S feet were plentiful and noisy. For once, Wolf stayed close by, nosing through every clump of withered grass and dying plant, no doubt hoping to find something disgusting to roll in. The cold sky was clear and slate colored, softened only by a plume of smoke in the distance that must be coming from Jo and Callum's. Gray had been wrong about snow arriving overnight, but correct in his belief that when summer finally ended, the fall would be abrupt.

It was nearing the end of October, but felt more like November or even mid-December, temperature wise. And while Gray was used to the region's extreme weather fluctuations, Mia was not. He smiled, knowing full well she'd greet him with a rundown of the temperature—how cold it was, how the speed of the transition was "bizarre," and how she still couldn't believe she'd been swimming outside just three weeks ago. She religiously avoided referring to the aquatic adventure where they'd first met as skinny dipping, and he didn't harass her about it because he was constantly doing his best to keep the memory of her, wet and naked in the sunlit water, from the forefront of his mind. He didn't need to be fighting wood every time he worked with her. But it was hard. Pun intend-ed.

"Well, don't you look happy about something," Mia said, popping out of the forest and joining him on the trail. She'd taken to doing this lately, hiking to meet him on their scheduled days, instead of waiting for him to show up.

"Do I?"

"Yes. You're . . . *smirking*. I've never seen you do that before. What were you thinking about?"

Nope, not going there. He'd go to his grave first. "I'll never tell."

She rolled her eyes and turned her attention to Wolf. Gray really liked that now that she knew the dog better, she talked to Wolf the same way he did. "And how are you today, big fella? What's that? Oh yeah? You're tired of Gray pretending he has some deep, mysterious thought life the rest of us shouldn't be privy to?"

Okay, so maybe he only *sort of* liked how she talked to his dog.

Wolf stopped sniffing for a moment and raised his head, twisting it slightly so his left ear was angled up at Mia. She laughed. "Oh, I see how it is. You'll stop snuffling and snurfling long enough to let me scratch your ears?"

The mutt sighed with what seemed like intentionally comic exaggeration.

Laughter rumbled through Gray and he felt self-conscious. But come on, 'snuffling and snurfling'—how cute was that?

Mia stopped rubbing Wolf's head and stared. "Seriously, what is with you today?"

Gray shrugged. "Nothing." Then he took advantage of her being off guard and conversational. He dropped his pack and charged. Mia didn't waste a breath shrieking or giving any verbal show of surprise or acknowledgement of the attack. Her body veered slightly left and Gray followed the movement, reaching for her. With invisible speed, she switched gears and lunged right. Gray shifted direction too, but a fast, clever foot kicked out. He tripped and went sprawling—and hadn't even come close to getting a chance to grab the leg that took him down. All the years Mia had spent in dance lessons seriously showed in her light, feinting movements and ability to redirect her body instantly. He scrambled up and bolted after her, but she'd gotten a good fifteen or twenty paces lead. He stopped moving, brushed leaves and bits of tree debris from his cargo pants, and started to clap. She paused at the sound, then made her way back to him, jogging slowly.

"Not bad," he said.

She rubbed her forearms briskly. "And it helped me warm up. I can't believe how cold it's gotten—and practically overnight."

Gray laughed out loud again, and she gave him another odd look. "You'd better be careful, Gray. The way you're acting, I'm going to start thinking you enjoy spending time with me."

If only she knew. He feigned a casual vibe he didn't feel and grunted, "Just keep telling yourself whatever you need to get through the day."

She jabbed a light punch at his chest, then bobbed and weaved ahead of him, shadow boxing. He shook his head. "You're not going to become one of those people who take a few classes and develop a falsely inflated view of their abilities, are you?"

"No." She stopped bopping around, immediately. "Not at all. I like your fight till you're free then run philosophy."

Gray nodded and retrieved his backpack, both relieved and a bit sad that his sternness had made her serious again.

"So are you pleased with what you've learned so far?" he asked as they neared Sockeye cabin.

She sat down in one of the Adirondack chairs by the immaculate, unused fire pit. "This is lesson six, right?"

"Yep." They'd been meeting up regularly for two weeks, not counting their encounter in the Dining Hall, his visit to her cabin, or hers to his. It seemed impossible that they'd spent so much time together already, but the reverse was also true. In some ways it felt like they'd always known each other, no matter how carefully he tried to keep his guard up. Mia was a spontaneous, heart on her sleeve kind of person, or was the more he got glimpses of the real her anyway. Day by day, as she grew more and more relaxed in his company, the brittle, falsely chipper, overwhelmingly fearful person he'd first met showed up less and less. He knew it was a bad sign that he dwelled on the times they'd met in person—and a worse sign that he was already counting on more visits ahead.

"Well?" she said. "What do you think?"

"Sorry." He scuffed the loose gravel by the fire pit with his hiking boot. "I zoned out there. Do you mind repeating yourself?"

Her laugh tinkled like wind through a particularly pretty chime. "You really are out of it today. I said I think it's time. That maybe I'm ready."

Gray's whole body tensed. It was good news, of course, but what about him? Was *he* ready? "Okay, then. We'll take it really slow. If it starts to feel like too much or you start to panic, just say the word, all right?"

Chapter 13

WHEN GRAY GRABBED HER WRIST, Mia shuddered and all her limbs seemed to disjoint, making resistance impossible. She forced herself to breathe through it.

"You okay?"

She nodded. He released her and they stood without touching for a minute or two, then he clamped his hand around her other wrist. After a few repeats of this catch and release game, he grabbed both wrists. She froze and her insides sloshed in a hot queasy mess. No question, this was much worse.

"Okay?" he repeated.

She bit her lip, then bobbed her head. Another second passed and she was free again.

"I know it's stupid," she said, sides heaving like she'd been doing a grueling workout, not merely standing in one place for twenty minutes as Gray took hold of her hand or wrist, then let go, and repeat, repeat, repeat. "I totally know you're safe, but—"

"It's not stupid. A stress reaction isn't something a person can consciously control, without work. The body has its own memory, separate from the brain's."

That was definitely true. But what confused Mia was how these completely innocuous bits of contact made her feel like she'd regressed. She'd become totally fine during their non-touching workouts—even cocky. Now, even while chanting over and over in her head that the hand on hers was Gray's and that he was helping her, she felt trapped, like Ryland was right there again and she'd never—

"Hey." Gray's voice was gentle but firm. "Come back to me, Mia. Everything's fine. You're at your cabin. You're safe. Take a breath. That's right. There you go."

Mia inhaled, held the breath, then slowly expelled it, trying to squash down an upwelling of humiliation. "I know the stuff I need help with isn't even really self-defense."

Gray shrugged. "It is what it is."

At his cabin, after he agreed to work with her, she had been beyond relieved he didn't back out upon hearing exactly what she had in mind. For three whole sessions, all they'd done was practice her running away—with only words as a prompt, not even feigned contact. Then they'd moved to him lunging at her or pretending to try to grab her—but still without contact. She was planning to do the real, normal stuff you'd learn in regular self-defense classes, but first . . .

She inhaled and exhaled again, loudly. Gray hadn't acted like it was weird of her at all, but it was so embarrassing. She literally needed her hand held. She couldn't bear to face any moves that would demand close physical contact until she could manage to have someone hold her wrist or arm without having a meltdown.

"Stop it," Gray said, as if hearing her thoughts. "You're doing great."

"Oh, yeah, *great*," she replied bitterly. "I don't understand my glitch. If I can't stand to be touched without losing it, shouldn't that help me be able to get away, motivate me?"

"I can see why you think that, but what you're really working on is not getting yanked back into the night of the attack and being paralyzed by memories every time someone randomly touches you."

"I guess."

"Also, you don't ever need to apologize to me or try to defend or explain yourself. What you want to work on is specific and unique to you. Call it whatever you want, whatever feels most beneficial to you."

Mia liked that, the idea of labeling things in a way that felt beneficial to her. She appreciated the experts who helped her learn to cope by providing identifying terminology and explanations for things she experienced. Knowing her reactions and issues were direct, common responses to trauma or whatever, and being able to call them something specific was often useful, even comforting. Other times, however, she felt any type of professional jargon or "official" terms were euphemistic attempts to reduce messy, complex, destroyed parts of her into manageable, socially acceptable things. She wanted to reject every description she was supposed to select on mental health assessments and burn every tied up with a bow diagnosis. She appreciated how Gray didn't seem to think she was foolish for wanting to come up with the next phase of her own cure. Her own way.

A hand shot out and grabbed her wrist. She yanked free without giving it a thought. Then stared at Gray in surprise.

His brown eyes twinkled and his mouth, more visible these days since he'd started trimming his wild beard, quirked. "See? And that's after a mere half hour."

She nodded.

"So what do you think? Do you want me to rest my arm around your shoulder or put you in a light headlock?"

The idea made her stomach hurt. "How do I cue you if it's too much?"

"Just say so. I'll use a very, very light touch."

Gray stepped behind her just as Wolf bounded into view from around the side of the cabin. Mia was used to the dog's disappearing and reappearing acts now and tried to joke. "See? Wolf heard you and decided he'd better make sure you don't try anything funny."

"I will never try anything I don't run by you first. I promise." Gray's voice was soft and serious, and when something that felt like screws seemed to untighten in

Mia's stomach, she realized that maybe a small part of her *hadn't* been joking, had needed further reassurance.

She could sense Gray's physical presence behind her now, and he was so much larger, so much bulkier than she was. He was doing this to help her, sure, but if he wanted to overpower her, what—

"So, I'm going to put my arm lightly around your neck and count to three. Then I'll release you. It might feel scary, but remember, you're in control of whether I do this or don't, and sometime soon you'll be able to free yourself from someone you're not in control of."

It really was like he could read her mind—so maybe she shouldn't worry about this part of the lesson, she should worry about some of the other thoughts she had when he was near. A smile touched her face for the first time since starting the day's practice. "Okay. Go."

Gray must've speed counted because it was over before she even felt nervous. They practiced again and again and again, going for longer and longer periods of time, with him tightening his hold sometimes. Then they did the arm around the shoulder. It was a piece of cake compared to the choke hold. Despite the deodorant Mia was wearing, she could smell her own sweat when they were done.

"I'm sorry," she said when Gray undraped his arm for a final time and stepped away.

"About what?"

"I stink."

He laughed, but his eyes were serious. "Yeah, you do," he admitted in a low purr, "but I like it." He looked shocked by his own words and the tip of his nose and his ears reddened. Mia was sure any heat he was feeling was no match for the fiery warmth pooling through her limbs and belly, however. What a thing to say . . . and so strangely erotic.

Their eyes locked, but unlike other times where one or both of them immediately glanced away, they held each other's gaze, firmly, almost questioningly.

Mia broke first. "Um . . . " She took a step back and grabbed her phone from the arm of one of the Adirondacks. "Whoa, look at time. It's 3:30 already."

"Really?" Gray sounded surprised too. They'd been planning to keep sessions to under two hours. "I should split. It's a long way back." He stood up and shrugged into his backpack.

Mia watched him adjust the straps and fasten an extra support belt around his waist. "What do you keep in that thing anyway? And why do you wear it every-where?"

"You mean in my backpack?"

"Yeah."

"Just the basics in case I run into trouble on the trail." He shot her an almost angry look—a familiar expression that always made her laugh now that she was used to him. He was definitely gearing up to give her a safety lecture.

"And if you're still bent on traipsing around out here by yourself, you should make sure you're carrying survival essentials too."

He misread her smile—which was pure happiness that she'd successfully stalled him for a bit. "It's no laughing matter. Do you know how many accidents and events end in tragedy, when they should've gone down as fun adventure stories to recall over a beer, except that people are idiots?"

"No clue, but I bet you're going to tell me."

Gray grinned grudgingly. "Well, at least you know that much."

It was another thing she liked about him. He seemed aware of how owly and grumpy he could be, and while that awareness didn't stop him from compulsively launching into a lecture whenever something pressed his worry button, it did make his rants sort of sweet and endearing.

"Survival essentials?" she prodded.

"Yeah, ten things you should carry if you're going into the bush, no matter how short a hike you think it will be or how familiar you are with the terrain."

"And they are?"

"A light daypack is critical—I have a big sucker for extended trips—and you should leave it stocked so you can just pick up and go." He sat down on the wide arm of the Adirondack chair closest to her.

Though it was true Mia initially asked about the backpack only to keep Gray's company a while longer, now she found she was genuinely interested. She was going for longer and longer walks every day, and she had wondered what she'd do if she twisted an ankle, took a wrong turn, or even just got caught in unexpected weather.

"There's a ton of gadgets folks will try to sell you, but if you carry these ten, you'll be pretty set for most things," Gray said, warming to his topic. "Number one priorities: a knife—I prefer a fixed blade, but even a utility tool with a folding blade is better than nothing. Waterproof matches and/or a lighter. Water—or a container and something to purify water. Out here there's always a water source, but some places aren't like that and you'd need to pack bottles. Rope—I recommend parachute cord. A toque. I don't care how warm a day seems, temperatures always dip at night."

Mia nodded seriously, taking mental notes, trying to record everything he was saying.

"Signaling equipment. Obviously, a fire is a good one and I already mentioned matches—but a whistle, a mirror, a flashlight—I consider those all pretty critical. A compass and/or paper maps. A First Aid Kit, pretty self-explanatory. Shelter building equipment—which can be as simple as a tarp or large garbage bag. I also carry a light waterproof reflective blanket." Gray took a breath and studied her face, as if trying to deduce whether she was listening properly.

"That's nine main items, including the backpack—what's the tenth?"

Gray nodded approvingly, if a bit hesitantly, like he thought she might be teasing him. Either way, he was unable to resist completing his talk. "Finally, a change of clothes, in case you get wet or the temperature falls, so you can add layers."

Something Mia had heard somewhere popped into her head. "Aren't you forgetting something?"

Gray's brow creased. "Well, I carry a bunch of other stuff too, personal preferences, like a book and a notepad and pen, but no, that's a solid set of basics."

"What about a buddy? I thought experts always recommend not to hike without a partner."

For a second, Mia worried she'd gone too far. She'd only been teasing, but considering Gray's past, maybe her comment was insensitive. Then relief flooded her as he flashed a rueful smile and cocked an eyebrow. "In a perfect world, that'd be nice all right—but perfect's already eluded you and me. We're more like survivalists."

Mia was ridiculously flattered to be included in Gray's small club.

"Okay, till Tuesday then." Gray got to his feet again and whistled for Wolf.

Mia watched his departing . . . backpack. Five nights, four whole days until their next session. It seemed so long. "Hey Gray, wait."

He stopped obediently and she jogged over to him.

"I just wanted to say . . . thanks for everything. I really appreciate you making time and coming all this way to help me."

He smiled, then shrugged. "No biggie. I'm glad you're finding the lessons helpful."

She nodded, wanting to say more, but had no idea what that *more* was.

There was another pause, then as Gray made to step forward again, Mia stopped him once more, raising her hand, palm out.

He looked at her quizzically and maybe with a smidge of amusement.

"Spontaneous high five-slash-touch?" she asked.

His expression was definitely amused now. *Definitely.*

"Oh, yeah, very spontaneous." He raised his hand obligingly and their palms connected with a gentle smack—then stayed resting against each other.

Mia was shocked by the ripple effect of that simplest of touches. Was appalled by the fireball of need that ignited in her belly at the sensation of his callused palm pressed against hers. Yet it wasn't the thrill of sexual tension that threatened to undo her. Gray knew her, perhaps better than anyone now, especially regarding the darker details of some of her damage and fear, but his eyes weren't wary or filled with burdening concern. They were fond.

Gray's hand slid lightly up and down hers. This was a completely different thing from their workout touches—a whole new animal. How long had it been since Gray had touched or been touched by another human out of affection? As long for him as it had been for her? She felt like she was glowing with transparent excitement, even while she shuddered at the idea of wanting, of desiring, anything that could ever possibly hurt her again.

How could something as tame as two hands meeting in friendly camaraderie be so charged? It stoked a need in Mia that ran far deeper than physical desire, and mutual longing kindled in Gray's warm eyes.

He searched her face so unguardedly it was like he was touching her, slipping through layers, reading her, knowing her, *accepting* her just as she was. Bashful discomfort—and undeniable pleasure—tingled across her flesh. And then Gray's free hand stretched toward her. Soft as a butterfly's wing, he stroked her cheek.

Mia's breath caught. Gray winced. Then he smiled slowly, and her lungs filled with air again.

"Okay," she said, echoing his earlier words a little shakily—and a lot confused. "Till Tuesday it is."

"Yeah," Gray replied, sounding equally unsteady. "If anything comes up, leave a note in the tree."

Chapter 14

GRAY REACHED INTO THE HEART of the Secret Keeper, touched the unmistakable texture of an envelope and felt his blood surge. Was it another note from Mia? He couldn't help but hope wildly—and it wasn't beyond the realm of possibility. Despite their spending time together three times a week, or perhaps because of it, they occasionally wrote each other small letters. Silly things, really. She had a penchant for lame jokes and riddles, where she'd write out the question, then put the answer really small and upside down so he had to flip the note to read it. The first joke she'd sent hadn't included anything else, just the joke—something that made him chuckle much more than her offered groaner:

> What did the Tin Man say when he got ran over by a steamroller?
> "Curses! Foil again."

His reply had been a bundle of dried lavender and mint (wrapped in tin foil because yes, he was *that* hilarious and witty these days) along with instructions to take a hot soak and a promise that the combo would relax stiff muscles and ease anxiety.

They continued on from there, sharing random thoughts and quirky details from their solitary days.

His favorite note from her to date read:

Did you see the moon last night? I still can't believe how big and low it was, like if I walked just a few steps I'd be able to reach out and rest my hands on it. It made me feel both infinitely small and strangely powerful and resilient.

It was weird to think you might be watching it too, maybe even wrapped in a blanket, sitting in a chair beneath the inky sky, like I was—and it seemed odder still that strangers all over the place could see it too—because it felt intimate. Like magic or God is real and was reaching out to me personally.

(Yes, surprise! Another note from your insane friend!)

He had written back:

I know what you mean. Living out here, so close to nature in its most pure state, unsullied by other humans, has made me conscious of how insignificant I am in the larger scheme of things—but also how tied into it I am—how tied into it we all are. And not just when the moon's out.

My life, while everything to me, is a pebble on the river's floor, tumbling in the current. My pain, while huge to me, is one rain drop in the millions falling on the lake, barely making a ripple. And my joy is a star in the night sky, brilliant and beautiful and seemingly transcendent—but even while I'm experiencing it, long past and burnt out. Some people would find that depressing. I take comfort in it. The earth beneath me, the trees around me, the mountains above me have been here since time immemorial—and will still be here when I'm no longer even a memory. I am the tiniest part of something bigger than myself, something that will continue on with or without me, immune to my actions or demise.

Gray thought of signing the note with something like "Equally Insane," but in the end left off with three lines from an Emily Dickinson poem instead:

I'm Nobody! Who are you?
Are you – Nobody – too?
Then there's a pair of us!

Mia hadn't replied to that one yet and his hands shook with expectation as he broke the seal on the unmarked envelope. He hadn't even realized how much he missed conversing about the strange musings that moved through his head until she'd opened up this line of communication. And he wasn't obtuse—at least, not about this. He knew not everybody pondered such things—or maybe they did, just didn't talk about it. Either way, their note passing was something special, something unique, like Mia was, as he was becoming more and more aware. It made her danger-ous—the way she opened the empty places in him and made him crave to have them filled—but he couldn't muster the discipline to stay away.

Without warning or even a hint he was hovering nearby, Simon bounced into Gray's mind, grinning impishly, voice inquisitive and eager. "Whatcha doing, Dad?" he asked—his favorite question.

So real Gray couldn't help but return the smile and breath, "Hey, kiddo." He almost reached to tousle his son's hair—and memory, *reality*, smashed into him like nail-spiked baseball bat, breaking flesh, bruising vital organs, stinging and nauseating.

Gray staggered under the new assault of old loss. He closed his eyes against the familiar pain, and dropped onto a weathered log, its protective bark long gone, its aged body beaten smooth and featureless by time. Simon's question reverberated through him. What *was* he doing? Playing with gasoline and a match, that's what.

His pleasure in the letter blown to smithereens,

Gray slowly withdrew and unfolded the solitary sheet of paper.

Then he took in the first line of writing and froze. Jo's penmanship not Mia's. And glaringly formal. A siren of alarm screeched through him.

Dear Gray,

A woman named Tracy Kegan called, trying to get ahold of you. Her husband has passed away, and she's afraid you didn't know that he'd been sick. She'd like you to fly out.

Don't worry about waking me and Callum up. Pack a bag and come as quickly as you can at any hour. We'll drive you to the airport and see about you getting a standby flight. The Celebration of Life is on Sunday.

I'm so sorry for your loss (and for these absolutely meaningless words),

Jo

The Celebration of Life. Gray's mind balked at the phrase. Wouldn't process it. Funeral. Jo meant *funeral.* But that didn't make any sense. That meant Kip was dead. And Kip wasn't dead. He couldn't be. Just because Gray thought he'd made peace with the idea of his own inevitable passing didn't mean that he accepted the travesty when it happened to others—the stream of nonsense masquerading as philosophy sputtered to a stop. Kip had died. Of some illness Gray hadn't even known about. It must've come on quickly—or the diagnosis had, anyway—because Gray had talked to him five months ago and he'd been fine. Gray closed his eyes. Accidents, guns, bombs—and even if you could avoid those things—sickness or old age. No one you loved escaped.

He slowly refolded the note, returned it to its envelope, and slid it gently into his pocket. His limbs were leaden, his brain sluggish.

Back at his cabin, his rucksack practically packed itself. He dumped a full bag of feed in his chickens' automatic feeder and filled two waterers, instead of the usual one. Then he whistled for Wolf, filled a bucket with kibble for him and told him to stay. The dog wouldn't comply completely, no doubt, but he wouldn't follow him across the river, at least, and he'd half-ass guard the place.

As Gray hurried along the most direct route to Jo's, traveling by moonlight because it allowed his eyes to adjust and see in the shadows in a way that a flashlight didn't, he recalled Mia's words about the moon. Acid rose in his throat and he paused, feeling he might vomit. He was spared that, but the bitter heaviness didn't pass. What had he been thinking, letting himself get remotely close to her? It was a recipe for nothing but pain.

The shelter of the trees diminished, revealing the moon that lit his way and tortured his thoughts—not full and close this night, but thin and waning. Gray broke into a halting jog, his breath trailing behind him, white as a shroud in the darkness.

The nearer he got to River's Sigh B & B, to *Mia*, the further he distanced himself in his head. He almost wished he'd never met her. He'd been fine, more than fine—as near to happy as he could ever expect to be now—before she disturbed his corner of the woods. Perhaps it was a shame that he wasn't a stronger man, but he couldn't be what he wasn't. He wasn't up to letting another person close, only to have them leave or worse. It would be an adjustment to isolate himself again, but he'd do what he needed to do.

Chapter 15

MIA PACED SOCKEYE'S STONE TILE floor and cracked her knuckles, trying not to study Jo's face too intensely while she talked, not wanting to give away her worry and sadness for Gray.

"So," Jo continued, "that's pretty much it. He said to apologize for being a no show and to tell you he'll be back in a week or so. He knows the clock is ticking on your time here, so he understands if you want to continue the work you've been doing with someone else in town."

Mia shook her head tersely, not trusting herself to speak. She hated the selfish disappointment seeping through her. Yes, it sucked that her time with Gray would be put on hold indefinitely, but what really bothered her was that he hadn't taken the time to jot even the shortest note of explanation *himself*. The fact that it bugged her made her feel like the biggest jerk in the world. The poor man had already lost so much and now, according to Jo, he had lost his best childhood friend.

Of course, Mia didn't expect him to reach out to

her in his grief, but she couldn't help wishing he had. Awareness hit with an unpleasant jolt. Gray was the first person *she'd* want to share any news or concerns with, big or small, like her new camping backpack and all her safety goodies, even though they hadn't known each other that long.

A brisk rap on Sockeye's door interrupted Mia's thoughts before they fully registered.

Jo's chin lifted. "Are you expecting someone?"

"No," Mia said without moving. Then she realized that Jo expected her to answer the door, of course, not to ignore whoever was there. Stomach rolling, she crept forward as another knock sounded.

Happily—and surprisingly—her anxiety dissipated as soon as she opened the door. Sam stood there in soft knee-high boots and a gorgeous moss green sweater that brought out the twinkle in her jade eyes.

"I heard the resident wild man has headed for other parts and thought you might want to go shopping."

It was impossible to resist Sam's mischievous grin or the opportunity to distract herself from her weird feelings regarding the "wild man," a description Mia felt was ill fitting. Gray was only a little bit wild—and besides, "wild" was nowhere near as unattractive as Sam made it sound. Nowhere near at all.

Before she could utter a hearty "I'd love to," one of Sam's beautifully arched eyebrows rose. "Oh my . . . are you *blushing*? About the wild man?"

"Um, no, not at all."

"Um, no, *not at all*," Sam parroted cheerily. "Me thinks thou dost protest too much—or are you saying you don't want to shop?"

Mia laughed croakily and shrugged. "I'd love to go to town, Sam. Thanks."

Sam linked her arm through Mia's. Mia jumped and yanked away hard. For the briefest moment, Sam looked surprised. Then she smiled as if there hadn't been an awkward moment to speak of. "How about it, Jo? Are you joining us too? We could make it a girls' day out."

"I'd love to," Jo said, "but I've got someone coming to look at the septic field."

Sam's hands flew up in a delighted gesture. "Oooh, *lucky*. How glamorous!"

Mia giggled. The woman never quit.

"Yep, it's the life, all right." Unlike Sam, Jo didn't sound sarcastic in the least, and Mia was pretty sure she meant it, septic fields and all.

"Your loss. Mia and I are going to talk and talk— and she's going to spill all the juicy details about her and Grizzly Gray."

"Another time." Jo shot Mia a teasing look. "If you survive this one, that is."

"That's assuming we'll extend another invitation."

"Of course we will," Mia said.

"Oh, quit sucking up—and meet in the parking area in an hour?"

Mia nodded. "Sounds great."

Sam opened the door, Jo on her heels, then stopped and pivoted toward Mia again. "I totally forgot. I'll have my little granddaughter with us, just for an hour. Her mom has a meeting in town and asked if I could keep her for a bit, then drop her off. Is that all right?"

"Of course," Mia said. "I'd love to meet her, though I can hardly believe you're old enough to be a grandmother."

"Because I'm definitely *not* old enough, that's why—though being a grandma is the best thing ever. If a person can swing it, I highly recommend it."

"Sam's granddaughter is Mo, and Mo's mom is Aisha, my niece," Jo explained.

Mia nodded. She had put it together already, though it struck her as odd that Sam referred to Aisha as her granddaughter's mom, not by name or not just as her daughter. It made her curious about Sam and her story.

Jo apologized again for not coming with, Sam re-confirmed their meet up time, and Mia shut the door behind them, anticipation and dread warring within her.

On the one hand, it would be so fun to browse shops, go for lunch and chat with a friend, like normal people did all the time. On the other hand, she wasn't all that normal anymore and hoped she wouldn't have a meltdown. She was also extremely uneasy about Sam's glib "Mia and I are going to talk and talk" comment. She didn't want to talk about Gray. A) There was nothing to say, and B) *There was nothing to say.*

It turned out, however, that Mia had worried needlessly. For all of Sam's teasing and comical posturing, Mia found her remarkably easy to hang out and be herself with. They had a lovely time with Mo, a sweet, smiley-faced imp who had just added the word "Whoa" to her vocabulary. She uttered it non-stop, with an endless variety of enunciation.

A bright red toy firetruck with an extendable ladder and loud siren, spotted in the drugstore, received a "Whoa, whoa, whoa!" Each "whoa" in the trio, short and clipped, almost a yip.

A fruit smoothie with whipped cream and a cherry, purchased from a vendor in the library park and placed in her chubby hands by Grandma Sam got an appreciative "*Whoa*," so soft and drawn out, it was barely breath.

When a car screamed past them, driving too close to the sidewalk and too fast for downtown, it was a commanding bark: "Whoa!"

And for no seeming reason at all, for a good part of their trekking about, she chanted, "Whoa, whoa, whooooooa," under her breath in a cheerful, slightly awed tone, like being out and about with her grandma and her grandma's friend was the best, most amazing thing ever.

Mia's face hurt from smiling and she suspected Sam's did too. The little girl definitely had her Grandma's whole heart. As they waited for a light to change so they could cross the street to the place Aisha was meeting them, Mia asked, "Is she always this happy and good?"

Sam nodded, her face wistful. "Yes. Miraculous, hey? She reminds me a lot of Jo."

"I guess, but I definitely see a lot of you in her too. She's smart, funny—already totally aware of her audience—and up for anything."

Sam's smile broadened into a grin. "Oh, don't flatter me. I usually get my audience all wrong. Ask Jo."

"You guys are close, hey?"

"I'm impressed you noticed. Not everyone sees it, or appreciates my . . . sparkling wit."

Mia laughed.

"Jo, no matter how much I tease her, and my husband Charlie are the kind of people who remind you that good still exists in the world. They make me optimistic for monkey here." Sam nodded down at Mo, who was singing under her breath and skipping to and fro—or as far to and fro as she could anyway, with Sam holding her hand. "She's a good one too."

"And your daughter, Aisha, I mean . . . is she a 'good one'?" Mia was shocked at her prying question and wanted to swallow it back, but it was too late.

Before Sam could reply and just as the walk signal flashed, a little storefront caught Mia's eye. "You guys go. I'll catch up."

Sam looked quizzical but nodded.

"Walk!" Mo informed them, and she and Sam

heeded the command, crossing the street without Mia.

Mia strode over to the shop. Its darkened display window was decorated with the sparkling silhouette of a huge saxophone and a trail of glittery musical notes. She traced her hand along one. Practically nothing more than a hole in the wall, the little store looked like it had been closed for a while. When Mia leaned close to the glass, however, framing her eyes with her hands to see better, she realized it was still fully stocked. A handwritten note taped to the inside of the glass door grabbed her attention. She hesitated for barely a second, then pulled out her phone and snapped a picture.

Breaking into a swift run, she caught up with Mo and Sam at the next corner, just as Sam swooped Mo up and over a huge puddle by the curb. Mo was still giggling when Sam set her safely on the sidewalk again and glanced over at Mia. "To answer your question . . ."

Mia shook her head, half amused, half apologetic, as Sam continued their conversation like it hadn't even paused, "Aisha is one of the *great* ones. The only problem is that she sees me a little too clearly, without the kind, rose-colored glasses her dad and my sister—and apparently you—view me through."

"So you guys aren't close?"

Sam shrugged, but her expression was almost too nonchalant. Mia suspected it was a carefully manufactured poker face. "We're not *not* close—but she had a wonderful mother who died too young and I'm not her, so it's complicated. However, she accepts that I'm her dad's wife and lets me love up my grandbaby. I have more than I ever expected I would."

Before Mia could embarrass herself with another digging question, they arrived at a small office bearing a sign that read "Community Futures."

A young woman, the spitting image of Jo, wild curls and all—but with Sam's fair coloring and almost white blond hair—was slouched against the office's exterior wall, out of view of its window, face downcast.

Concern nipped Mia. The girl had to be Aisha, but she looked so . . . . pensive at best, totally discouraged at worst.

Mo caught sight of the woman and burst into a happy dance. "Whoa, Mom!"

The woman's head jerked and an instant smile seemed to tug her whole body up along with it. "Whoooa, Mo!" she replied.

Mo chuckled like her mom had made the best joke ever.

Mia studied Aisha as she scooped Mo up and nuzzled her neck. Had she misread her earlier body language? Sam's question made her think not.

"Bad news?" she asked.

Aisha stopped lavishing attention on Mo, glanced at Sam, then shrugged. "Not exactly, but not good either. I might qualify for this new grant program, but I need a better business plan—and apparently I have competition. Someone with an idea similar to mine contacted them recently."

"I can help you if you want," Sam said, more hesitant than Mia had ever heard her.

"I'm good," Aisha said shortly—then seemed to catch herself. "Thanks, Sam. I appreciate all you do with Mo, but other than that, I want to do this on my own."

Sam nodded, kissed Mo good-bye, and then Aisha and Mo were on their way.

As Sam and Mia commenced walking again, Sam let out a heavy sigh. When she spoke though, her tone was flippant. "Kids!" she exclaimed, then whistled. "They're exhausting. Thank goodness I didn't meet her until she was seventeen."

There was nothing really to say to that and Mia wondered if she and Sam were going to lose the casual loveliness of their day without little Mo to act as a buffer and easy source of conversation. Again, her fears were quickly put to rest.

"So you prodded my soft spots, now it's my turn," Sam said as they headed to a shoe store she lauded as being "surprisingly great."

"Okay . . ." Mia said. She had so many obvious issues. Which one of her pathetic neuroses would Sam target?

"Why don't you play guitar anymore?"

Whatever tender area Mia expected Sam to poke, it

wasn't that. Unfortunately, before she could ask how Sam even knew she no longer played, their day did get wrecked—and in a way that Mia hadn't seen coming and hadn't even thought to worry about.

Chapter 16

"*OH. MY. GOD!*" THE SHRIEKED words came from someone Mia didn't see at first, but something in the speaker's shrill excitement and volume set her teeth on edge. Seconds later, a flushed faced woman with red hair and dark roots, shoved past Sam.

"Hey," Sam exclaimed, but was ignored.

"You're Mia Clark. *The* Mia Clark. It's Mia Clark!" The stranger announced to the world, causing other foot traffic to pause, blocking Mia and Sam's entry to the shoe store.

"Who?" someone asked, looking straight past Mia. The question shattered the spell and the small crowd moved about their business again.

The woman, however, was not put off by the lack of response, and she had a companion. Mia felt like she was watching the scene unfold from under water, everything muted and wobbly, as she took in the rough-skinned man with a short buzz cut and an expensive looking jacket, who held the woman's arm. He checked Mia out in a repulsively obvious way, noticeably pausing at her hips and again at her breasts, before gawking at her face.

"I think you're right," he announced like Mia wasn't even there. "She's old now, but she's still a fox." He laughed like he was clever and funny, though he was neither. Mia's gorge rose.

"You have to give me your autograph!" Quick as a flash, the woman produced a pen and a small day planner from her purse. "My God," she said again. "How I *loved* you."

"Who didn't?" The man's grin was more like a leer. Mia tried to tell herself he might just be socially inept, not intentionally disgusting—but then he wet his lips in an exaggerated way with his fat tongue.

Mia felt dizzy. A few pedestrians slowed again, curiosity piqued anew. She needed the couple to go away. The fastest way to make that happen was to—

As if from a great distance, Mia saw herself reach for the pen, though everything inside her keened in resistance.

Suddenly a smooth, pretty hand with a square-tipped French manicure snatched the pen from her and thrust it back at the woman. It was Sam to the rescue. She rolled her eyes at the woman and spoke in a dry, slightly condescending tone. "Don't feel badly. You're not the first person to mistake my lunatic sister for Clark."

The woman's mouth dropped open, as Sam turned to Mia and hissed, "Are you insane? Seriously! Stop being such an imposter. It's embarrassing."

"You mean, she's not . . . what?" The woman looked at Sam, then at Mia. The fangirl awe that had glazed her expression seconds earlier morphed into a look of intense dislike. "How pathetic," she exclaimed. "You don't even look that much alike. I can't believe you go around masquerading as Mia Clark. Get a life."

What had just happened? Mia's brain practically shot off sparks as she jumped up to speed. "Um, so does that mean you don't want an autograph, after all?" she called to the woman's quickly departing back. Sam snickered.

The woman didn't slow, but the man in her grip did a half turn. "You could still autograph me, sweetheart."

"Gross, Carl," the woman said, yarding him back into line. From the outrage and indignation in her voice, a person would've thought Mia was the one who had accosted *them*.

Gross indeed. Couldn't have said it better myself, Mia thought. When the creepy couple were well out of hearing distance, she shot Sam a look, shaking her head in wonder.

"What?" Sam raised her hands as if confused. "Don't tell me you're put off by a little fib. We *could* be sisters. I mean, don't feel bad, I know I'm prettier, but you're not bad looking yourself . . . except you're old apparently."

Despite the waning adrenalin making her queasy, Mia laughed. "You're incorrigible!"

Sam grinned. "Now you really *do* sound like my

blood relation."

She linked her arm through Mia's and hauled her into the shoe store. As it had earlier in the day, Mia's whole body went rigid in Sam's grasp. This time she forced herself not to pull away. To let herself take comfort in it.

"Sam—" Mia broke off, at a loss for how to put her gratitude into words, but apparently Sam didn't require thanks. In fact, she seemed bent on avoiding it. She dropped Mia's arm to focus all of the considerable force of her attention on a pair of purple suede boots.

"Oh. My. God," she said in perfect parody of the horrible woman. Mia chuckled but it felt obligatory now, like she was playing the part of a woman enjoying an afternoon out with her zany friend, not a real person doing anything of the sort. "These boots are gorgeous—totally impractical for the weather up here. I'm getting them."

Trying to get back in the spirit of things, Mia asked the saleswoman if she could try on the purple boots too.

Sam's eyebrows shot up. "Copycat!" she exclaimed, but seemed delighted.

Mia adored the boots. The color reminded her of Sockeye's vivid door. They had flannel lined uppers, thick, comfy rubber soles, and fit like they'd been custom designed for her.

She and Sam made their way to the till together, boots in hand. Sam got hers wrapped up, but at the last minute, Mia changed her mind. She didn't need the boots, and really, what was the point? It wasn't like she'd go anywhere anyone would see them.

A frown creased Sam's face for a moment, but then she was her dry, cheery self again. "Your loss," she said lightly.

The rest of the afternoon only got flatter from there. The sense of fun and easy camaraderie she and Sam had enjoyed was gone, and Mia knew it was her fault. Sam chatted about this and that as they hit a grocery store to pick up a few things, then browsed through the marvelous magazine selection at the local independent bookstore. Mia tried to respond appropriately, but her heart wasn't in it.

Finally, over a late lunch of spicy Pad Thai at a little place called Don's, Sam lost patience with her.

"Those people were losers, hey? They totally wrecked our day."

"Yeah," Mia agreed sadly.

"Wrong." Sam set her water glass down so hard it made a banging sound. "You're wrecking it."

Mia nodded again. "I'm sorry. My mood's the pits, I know. I should've called it a day before we had lunch. I just thought, since we'd already planned it—"

"Nope, that's not what I'm saying either. I can handle a bad mood, or a sad mood, or a mad mood. What I don't like is this resigned *blah*. You ran into some jerks. So what?"

Mia's eyes smarted, but Sam wasn't done. "Newsflash; There are jerks everywhere—and it's not because you're Mia Clark. We could've just as easily had a run-in with some rude loser who had no idea who you are."

"I can't help it. Things like that are a trigger. They remind me of how bad I am at reading people and how I can never deal with things myself, or protect myself . . . What if you weren't there?"

Sam shrugged. "But I was. And there's no shame in accepting help from a friend. And if I wasn't there, big deal, you'd have signed the poor woman's planner."

"The *poor* woman?"

"She's attached herself to a man, and I use the term euphemistically, like Carl. Trust me, her life, and her issues, are worse than yours."

Sam had a point. "Yeah, okay, but—" Mia wanted to explain how incidents like this might not seem like a big deal to Sam, but each one blew itself up in Mia's mind, made her worry that this newest person wouldn't go away. Maybe they'd keep trying to contact her. Maybe they'd start following her or graft themselves into her life somehow. Maybe they already posed some threat she wasn't aware of . . .

Sam interrupted like she was psychic. "I'm not saying it's easy. I'm saying you need to stop giving your power to other people. Don't let a rotten five minutes wreck your whole day. Pretend you're brave until you actually are. Brazen it out—you know, the whole fake it till you make it thing."

Mia chewed her lip, noodles and shrimp forgotten. She didn't know if Sam's speech was the right thing to say to someone who'd been through what she had been. Usually people went overboard with sympathy. Told her how difficult, how almost impossible to get over, it must be. Even went so far as to agree that retreating from the world and keeping her circle small and limited to only the closest friends and family was, if not optimal, certainly sensible. And she appreciated that understanding. And maybe in the first year, Sam's "advice" would've fallen on deaf ears, or been too hurtful. Mia might've felt like Sam was saying her injuries were all in her head, were all a *choice*. Today, however, where she was *now*, she found herself liking Sam's hard ass, practical form of empathy—and her assumption that Mia could handle things.

"Also, I need to apologize to you."

Mia's attention jerked back to Sam. "What? No, you don't."

"Yes, I do. I lied back there—and I very rarely lie. A little omission or avoidance of a fact here or there, maybe. Or the tiniest misdirection, perhaps . . . but no outright *lies*."

Mia didn't laugh. She was honestly confused. What was this big lie Sam was confessing about?

Sam sighed. "I wanted to tell your, ahem, admirers to bugger off and/or to get some manners. That yes, you're Mia Clark, but you're not signing autographs—

but then I remembered Jo's command about secrecy."

"Oh . . ."

"That's right . . . *oh*. So I didn't feel I had the freedom to spill the beans officially by speaking my mind—but that's what you need to do. Learn to say No. Honestly, just repeat after me, 'No, I'm not signing autographs.' 'Step back.' 'Get away from me, cretin Carl.'"

Sam's words had their desired effect this time. Mia finally smiled a sincere smile again. Even chuckled a little.

Sam nodded encouragingly, and her miss-nothing green eyes were intense. "That's right, laugh. It *is* funny. Arm yourself with that laughter in public, keep up a shield of aloof reserve, and never let them see they've shaken you. I can't believe you never learned any of this, considering how much fan contact you must've had."

"My manager—my mom—and hired staff handled any ugliness. I just had to smile for fans' cameras and be nice to reporters. I never had to really talk or make hard decisions. Never wanted to. I loved the music. I could've done without everything else."

"That's rough." Sam sipped her black coffee, her own food untouched too. "I used to be bitter about not having anyone watch out for me when I was young, but sometimes I think it had some benefits too. At least I wasn't made weak and vulnerable by the best of intentions. No one raised me to be 'nice.' Yes, some people think I'm a big bitch, but I kind of recommend it. More women need to be able to say fuck off when the occasion—or person—warrants it."

Mia giggled like a nine-year-old when Sam's F-bomb exploded, and once she started, she couldn't stop for a long time.

"Is Jo as tough as you?" she asked when she could talk again.

"Tougher—but tell her I said so and die."

Mia shook her head.

"People think Jo's a pushover, but she's not. She's kind. It's different. No one fools her, and if they think they have, it's because she's letting them think it. She'll help anyone who needs it, regardless of who they are to her."

The description jarred Mia; it was very similar to how Jo had described Gray.

"So basically," Sam continued, "she's tough like I said *and* totally nauseating."

Mia nibbled a forkful of noodles, then took a bigger bite. The food was very good, but she was suddenly impatient to get moving again. "You've made me feel better, thank you."

Sam's voice was wry. "Not exactly what I was shooting for, since you need to be able to make yourself feel better—but good enough for now."

Mia shoveled down two more big mouthfuls of food, downed her water, and stood up.

"What on earth?"

"Hurry and finish your meal. I've got something to do that can't wait."

"Eating's for wimps." Sam stood too. "What's up?"

"SO ACTUALLY YOUR DAY DIDN'T get wrecked. It was wonderful," Mia corrected her negative thoughts aloud. "You had a rough ten minutes and let it color an hour or two. Big deal. The beginning and the end of the day were fabulous." She rested her legs on her cabin's funky coffee table, admired her new purple boots, and grinned, remembering Sam's expression when she realized what Mia's urgent "to do" was.

"You don't think it's too weird if I buy the same boots as you?" she had asked Sam, making sure before she dug out her credit card.

"Trust me, that's the least weird thing about you."

"True, that," Mia said happily, making Sam snort.

Recalling the moment, Mia was just as happy. She had hoped this trip would help her become her old self again—her old self or better. And maybe it was working. She'd even made a fast and true friend, something she never would've predicted. Before she'd arrived at River's Sigh, it had literally been years since she met anyone new without her mom and sister guarding her back. Now she had a whole crew of new acquaintances that she trusted.

Yes, she'd had an annoying clash with someone

who recognized her and had aggressively wanted something from her—and true, she hadn't handled it herself—but she'd seen it dealt with so casually and easily that she had high hopes of doing so herself in the future.

Most exciting of all, or, at least as exciting as everything else, was the lonely music shop in need of a new owner. The note on the door revealed it wasn't as small as it appeared to be. In addition to the retail storefront, it had a small studio in the basement and lesson rooms in the back. Was she nuts to even be considering it? She wanted a big change, a new scene, but—

Argh, there was so much twirling around in her head, good and bad.

She wanted to talk to Gray or to write him a note—or maybe a poem. Poems weren't lyrics. Or not exactly—and writing things to Gray didn't really count as *writing* writing, right? Well, maybe it did, but it didn't paralyze her the way contemplating writing songs again did. But Gray wasn't around. She couldn't hike over to see him. And it was nearly dark—not the best time to go to their tree.

To distract herself and hoping to burn off some energy, Mia called her sister. And got voicemail. She left a message.

"Jackie? Hello! It's me. Call me back. I have great news. I went up town, bought boots, ate lunch—and I have a new friend, or I should say, *we* have a new friend. You'll love her too. Also . . . I have an idea. Or a possible idea. Maybe. Call me back. Have I said call me back? I mean it. Call meeeeeee!"

Mia hung up and cranked her music, then danced around the room in her purple boots. For the first time in so long she couldn't remember how long exactly, she was locked away in the safe privacy of her little cocoon—and didn't want to be. Or not fully anyway. An increasingly loud part of herself wanted to be out and about. It was Friday night, guys. Friday night! She didn't want to party, exactly. That would never be her scene again—but dinner out would be nice. Or a concert.

The idea that she was contemplating such things with anticipation not dread was mind blowing. She dug out her journal, planning to diligently report her progress—but instead found herself trying to capture snippets of the thoughts and images streaming through her brain. She wouldn't call her scribblings lyrics or poetry or anything at all. She'd just let them out.

Chapter 17

"WHAT'S UP WITH YOU? SOMETHING'S different," Gray muttered almost to himself—but it was true. He'd only been gone a week and a half, yet Mia had . . . changed.

She looked surprised, then grinned sort of shyly and waggled her foot. "It's just the hot purple boots."

"It is not the boots," he groused. "But they're something else, all right."

"Something else good, or something else bad?"

Gray wasn't sure. He was too distracted by her denim clad legs—ah, that was part of the difference maybe. Her clothes. He was used to her baggy sweats and tucked up hair. Seeing her in snug jeans and a low-necked sweater was . . . disconcerting. He was already disturbingly attracted to her when she was in workout gear, sans makeup, sans effort. Now that she was dressing up, or he was around when she was dressed up anyway, he couldn't help but notice—and he didn't like it. Or rather, he *did* like it. That was the problem.

They were sitting on Sockeye's cozy covered porch with a crackling fire blazing away in the little chiminea. Over their heads, rain pounded a wild beat on the tin roof, streaming from the sky in sheets, not drops.

Gray tried not to think how nice it was to sit and watch the rain with Mia, rather than languishing at his place, listening to it alone. He'd been back for three days and this was his second time seeing her, despite the crazy rain, although they hadn't resumed lessons yet. He'd stopped by on his way home from the airport, ostensibly to check in with her and to confirm she hadn't started training with someone else, that she still wanted lessons from him. He knew better than to believe his own excuse though. He'd missed her while he was away. Grieving his friend, helping Tracy with arrangements, enduring the rigmarole of the funeral, etc.—none of it had kept his mind off her. And then today he'd come to see her, well, because he was weak and couldn't stay away.

"Back in a sec," she said suddenly, popping out of her seat and disappearing into the cabin. Gray tried not to watch her departure and failed miserably.

"You're scowling," she said, when she reappeared a few minutes later, carrying two steaming mugs of hot chocolate.

He set his down on the porch railing. "We have to talk," he said at the exact same time Mia chirped, "I'm so happy you're back!"

She obviously heard him because the warm glow in her eyes dimmed a bit.

"Talk about what?" she asked guardedly.

"The little notes, the impromptu visits, our hanging out longer than designated lesson times . . . It all has to stop."

Mia had been about to sip her cocoa, but now she lowered the brimming mug without a taste. "But why? I thought that we were, maybe, um . . ." Her cheeks flamed as she stumbled over her words, then she repeated herself and finished her sentence in an embarrassed whisper. "I thought we'd become friends."

Shit, thought Gray. That was the predicament, all right. They *had* become friends. Or maybe, as she'd sort of implied, even been on their way to flirting with something more. His memory replayed the sweet, awkward high five she'd given him. He knew now, as he had then, how much her voluntarily initiating physical contact meant.

He avoided her eyes. "My best friend since we were eight died last month. I hadn't seen him face to face in years—not since Celine and Simon's funeral—and I didn't call him enough." He had no idea why he added those last two bits of information.

"I know. Jo told me when she explained you'd be missing some of our sessions. I'm so sorry, Gray. I didn't bring it up because I figured you wouldn't want to talk about it, or at least not right away."

Astute of her. And kind. Two qualities that pretty much epitomized her. And if he did want to talk about it, it would be with her. The fact seared through him.

Gray crossed his arms over his chest. "You're right, I don't. But it reminded me, for a lot reasons, why you and I should keep a healthy distance. You're leaving soon. No good will come of complicating things. If you still want self-defense tips, we can keep meeting, but we should leave it at that."

Mia focused on her beverage again, first testing the temperature, then taking a large swallow. Was she going to ignore him? Was she preparing to argue? Was her lack of response a way of saying she agreed with him? He couldn't decide what he hoped for more—that she'd let his request stand, or that she'd call him an idiot and say it was too late, that they were already somehow involved and would have to see how it played out.

She had practically drained her whole mug when she finally lowered it to her lap, hands wrapped tightly around it. "Being a friend, having a friend . . . Would that really complicate things so unbearably?"

Yes, he wanted to yell. If the friend was you, *yes*. He didn't yell though. He didn't even speak. He just shrugged.

Her face was sad. "I guess that makes sense. I came out here, to solitude, to try to find my way back to some semblance of a life. You came out here, went a lot further even, to try to keep life from touching you again."

He didn't disagree with her. "I'm not trying to be a dick. It's just easiest." "Safest, you mean. No risk of getting hurt or of one of us wanting more than the other person does."

"Exactly." He could practically see cogs turning in her head as she considered his words.

She bit her lip. "I agree. Very wise." She stood and reached for his untouched mug, then sloshed its contents over the railing onto the hard ground. The cocoa mingled with the rain and was gone. "So I guess I'll see you here Monday at one?" she added, her back to him.

"Yes. Right. Good," he said.

He saw her nod, though she still wasn't facing him. She headed for the cabin's purple door.

"Mia . . ." Gray began, then faltered. He had no idea what he wanted to say. Or what he *could* say. He was only getting—and she was only giving—what he'd asked for.

Mia started at the sound of her name and turned. Even in the dusk's fading light, she had noticeably paled. Her voice was tight and uncomfortable. "I totally forgot. There's a new letter in the tree. I delivered it yesterday. Ignore it, and please don't worry. I won't send another."

He opened his mouth to tell her he was sorry, that she shouldn't feel self-conscious about the note, that his only "worry" was that he'd like it too much, but she waved a mug to silence him. "Seriously, Gray, I get it. We're good."

But they didn't feel "good." They felt distanced or

like strangers or something. But that's what he wanted, right? "Okay, then . . . till Monday."

Mia closed the door behind her, leaving him alone outside.

Gray slid his waterproof pants over his jeans, pulled his slicker on, and did up the hood. He whistled for Wolf. The dog didn't come. He whistled again. Still no luck. He was half way to the river when Wolf finally made an appearance, panting like he'd been running hard, his breath a steamy smoke in the rapidly cooling air.

Gray detoured to the Secret Keeper. If it was going to be their last secret communication, he should relish it, right?

Because it was nearly dark and the river was swollen with the heavy autumn rains, his preferred trek across the shallow part of the river was out of question—and no doubt would be until spring. Grateful for his rain gear, he took the longer route that incorporated the small makeshift bridge.

When he stepped out onto it, however, it seemed to sway a little. Gray paused, then took another cautious step. Did the boards beneath him give a bit? He bounced lightly where he stood, testing its strength, then took a few more tentative steps. Now everything seemed solid, but that didn't necessarily mean anything. Sometime in the next few weeks, he'd return in the daylight and make sure the bridge didn't need repair. And who knew? Maybe it was fine. He might be seeing danger where there was genuinely none.

Chapter 18

MIA STEPPED OUT ONTO THE porch, steaming coffee mug in hand, and savored the cold smoky air. She sighed with deep contentment. God, it was beautiful here. The words were a prayer, something Mia hadn't been able to do in a long, long time. She studied the mountains in the distance. They were cloaked in low-sitting clouds, and so gray in the strange netherworld light that was River's Sigh in late fall that they looked like ancient stone castles rising out of the mist. The thought sparked the idea for a song, but she didn't hurry to capture the lines. Gray had been right. Something had changed in her, or, more accurately, had reverted back. The words, the idea, would still be there when she was done sitting out here. Possibilities were once again never-ending.

It was like the massive rock of fear, anger and pain that had been weighting her down, holding her back, blocking her off to art, music, words, *life,* had shifted. She first consciously noticed the difference after the shopping day with Sam, though she was at a loss as to how such a nondescript moment—one pushy fan was nothing in the grand scheme of things, after all—could have such profound impact. But maybe it wasn't just that. Maybe it was the cumulative effect of everything she'd been doing. Maybe the day with Sam was merely the final shove necessary to move the boulder that had already been nudged loose, rocked back and forth over time by the support of her mom and sister, the work with her therapist, her completely fluky wisdom in coming here—and Gray.

Gray. Good to his word, he'd kept coming for lessons. Every day she dreaded the heavy snow that would cut him off from her and end their sessions. So far, though, the snow had held off and he'd been able and willing to continue walking in. She'd lost track of how many classes they'd had together now, but it was the end of November and she was supposed to be going home in two weeks. She was confident that in all but the most extreme cases, if someone grabbed her or pinned her or tried to hold her down against her will, she could bust free. Go for the tender bits hard and fast, then split. And she was a kickass runner. Now anyway. She was grateful to Gray. And she had tried to leave it at that, tried hard, except—

Gray. Bad to his word—but to her delight—he had *not* broken off their letter writing habit. At the end of their first workout after his big "We Shalt Not" declaration, he'd turned to her casually. "I couldn't just ignore that note of yours. Whenever you have time, there's a reply."

To her credit, she hadn't literally *run* to the Secret Keeper the minute he was out of sight. But she may have jogged. At a fairly fast pace.

You are lovely, and your words are more than I deserve—but not reciprocated. Sorry.

If that's all Gray had written on the blue-lined loose-leaf, their notes would've stopped as he had requested. But he had continued, after a six-line gap.

I had a box of wild crab apples that weren't going to keep over winter very well, so I made jelly the other day. I like preserving because if you follow the prescribed steps, you get pre-dictable results. In this case, first you make juice—and don't squeeze your jelly bag. It's important that you let the juice drip through at its own pace (best done overnight), or your jelly will be cloudy. Then you make your jelly, careful not to tinker with the recipe or it won't set properly.

As I'm writing this, twelve jars are resting on the table, catching the last dregs of the day's sun and glowing like polished amber.

It's not the life for everybody, but as I go about the work involved in meeting my basic needs—water, food, shelter—and one day turns into the next and the next, it's easy for me to imagine that I'm the solitary survivor of an apocalypse or something. I don't feel lonely. There is even beauty in it. Peace.

Without saying it in so many words, Gray had explained what he had to give Mia—and that it was all that he had. She found it a heartrendingly telling and perceptive note. In a way, after all, Gray *was* an apocalypse survivor. She still didn't know how yet exactly, but his whole world—his wife and child, his career, his friendships—had been destroyed. And he was living in the aftermath. Alone.

She was glad he found some beauty in his lifestyle, and even though she saw the flaws in it now and couldn't embrace it for herself—knew that it was grief and fear behind his desire for complete autonomy, not strength—she could appreciate that yes, it would be peaceful. It would feel safe. But he was a bit deluded saying that he wasn't lonely. If he wasn't, he wouldn't have written back. And his stated basic needs "water, food, shelter" left out other things that were equally basic human needs ... companionship, connection, personal growth ...

No matter. Gray was right about one thing. His way was safer. For both of them. After her initial embarrassment and disappointment softened, she wrote back, keeping her response light.

And so their odd communications continued. Quotes from books, poems, and songs. Shared snippets of dreams and what they might mean. Newsy tidbits like what you might write to your aunt—or would've if you and your aunt had corresponded 100 years earlier. Gray's lifestyle definitely harkened back to an older era.

Very cold today. Definitely needed wool socks. Too bad mine didn't dry on the line fully—toes were frozen stiff. Guess laundry will have to become an inside job again.

On November 11, one came that made Mia cry.

So this is Remembrance Day. Ten years ago I was marching in a parade, unable to stop smiling, inappropriate or not, because Celine was in early labor. Our little son, Simon Gregory Robertson, appeared minutes before midnight.

The world was made new when he came into it, and the best part of me left it when he did.

There was no rhyme or reason to the when, why or what either of them sent. Sometimes they replied specifically to something said, but more often it seemed that offering a similarly intimate observation or recollection—even if it was along completely different lines—was a more fitting response. Sometimes she sent two or three notes to Gray's one. Sometimes it was the reverse.

The only rule was that they never referred to their

notes when they were in person, not even to say there was one waiting, after that initial time when Gray made it clear that they wouldn't stop after all. The chance of a note, then the reading and relishing of a note, were the favorite parts of Mia's day, and she didn't try to pretend otherwise. They were also why she was such a good runner. If she was going running anyway, it only made sense to go to the tree, right?

Sinking into one of the Adirondack chairs, Mia pulled a wooly throw over her lap. She sipped her coffee, which had cooled to a perfect sipping temperature.

Gray.

Gray.

Gray.

She still hadn't told him about her interest in the music shop. The timing had never been right—but he was the only thing making her second guess her new brainchild and change of plans. And she couldn't let him.

She thought again of the supposed end date of her trip, of the fact that Jackie and her mom were expecting her return in two short weeks, back in plenty of time before Christmas. And she dwelled once more on the picture on her phone that had been lighting fires in her brain ever since she'd taken it, the day she was in town with Sam and Mo.

If asked, Mia would've been hard pressed to explain why today was the day she mustered her courage.

It was just time, simple as that. Past time, even. She'd known the instant she'd seen the little shop for sale and ran her finger along the sparkling notes on its lonely window, that it was the new project she'd been waiting for. In the new town she'd make home.

She dug out her phone and entered the number she'd long since memorized.

An elderly baritone filled Mia's ear. "Hello?"

"Hello, I'm looking for Keith Carlsen."

"You've found him. What can I do for you?"

Mia introduced herself and why she was calling.

Keith cleared his throat. "You're not some kid having me on, are you? It's a great little spot and was real good to me for thirty years. I'm tired of lookie-loos—"

"No, sir. I'm serious. I want to look at it first, of course, but if everything's in order, I'd like to buy it. Financing won't be an issue."

"Well . . . "

For an edge-of-her-seat minute Mia thought she was about to be told she couldn't have the store, that the man didn't want to sell after all.

"Well . . ." he said again. "If this isn't perfect timing. Just last night my nephew was pressuring me to clear everything out and sell the building, not the business." He cleared his throat again and Mia was moved by his ragged emotion. "I would've been sad to see it come to that."

"When's a good time to view it?"

"How about today? Give me an hour, then come by

any time. I'll go over, soon as I've called my nephew and rubbed his nose in this new development."

Mia laughed. "Whoa—you sure you don't want to wait to gloat until I've signed papers or something?"

Keith's low voice was absolutely serious. "If you're genuinely in the market for a music shop, you're going to take one look and fall in love. She's a gem."

"I already thought as much," Mia said truthfully. "I'm super excited."

Okay, so a hard-nosed deal seeker she wasn't. She'd broken the cardinal rule of buying real estate by showing her eagerness—ah, well!

She told Keith she'd see him soon, ended the call, and pressed the phone to her chest, happiness waltzing through her. Her fluttery heart was beating almost as fast as when she worked out with Gray and excited anticipation tinkled in every nerve. She wanted to squeal like a kid—then did. It was crazy that completely changing your life could take less than two minutes!

Still grinning, she called Jackie. It would be better to get her to break the news to their mom, so she'd be somewhat prepared when Mia chatted to her next. Jackie, at least, understood that it was normal for a grown woman, married or not, to live apart from her parents—something their mom, despite how truly great she was in a lot of ways, God love her, didn't get.

Mia spilled her news in a giddy rush.

"Wow—that's a lot to take in," Jackie said. "Are

you sure about this?"

"Absolutely. I think. No, I *know*. I'm excited about it, actually."

"Well, you've definitely sounded different, in a good way, the last couple times we've talked." Jackie's voice grew teasing. "In fact, it's made me wonder . . . this isn't all because of some guy, is it?"

It had been forever and a day since Jackie had teased Mia about romance or men.

Mia must've taken too long to reply because Jackie exclaimed, "Holy crap, it *is*. You've met someone."

Mia shook her head, which was stupid because Jackie couldn't see her. "This is not because of 'some guy.' I promise."

And it was true. "The guy" didn't have a clue about her plans—and Mia was nervous to share them, afraid he'd misinterpret them.

There was a beat of silence. Then Jackie chortled, "Saying your change of plans isn't *because* of some guy is *not* the same thing as saying that there *isn't* a guy."

Mia wouldn't let herself be pulled into talking about a romantic relationship that didn't exist, so she changed the subject. "Tell me what the kids are up to. I miss them."

"They miss you too," Jackie said, promptly forgetting all about any possible mystery man as she warmed to her favorite subject—her eight-year-old twins, Chase and Treja. "They'll be more disappointed than

Mom that you're not coming home."

Listening to Jackie chat on about the upcoming Christmas pageants and the kids' hilarious wish lists, Mia, for about the millionth time, wondered what her life would have been like if she hadn't been a child star, if her mom had just been her mom, not her manager, and if she was the sister who got to marry her high school sweetheart and have two kids instead.

Just before they wound up their call, Jackie asked one more time, "You're really, really sure about this? And you won't even visit until the new year?"

"I'll let you know. I'm tempted to come for Christmas—just for a few days, though. I'll have my hands full getting everything off the ground."

Mia thought Jackie had left the call and was about to hang up too, when Jackie's voice came again, very softly. "I'm so happy for you, Me-Me. You're finally back. And you're following your heart again. It's about time."

Jackie's use of her childhood pet name made Mia mist up a little. And yes, she agreed in her head. *I am. And it is.*

On that note, she ducked back inside, grabbed her bag and keys and headed out. Keith's shop—no, *her* shop—was awaiting!

Chapter 19

ONE WEEK TO GO. ONE week to go. One week to go. The words pounded in Gray's head in time to the beat of his boots on the trail, encouraging him and making him despair in turn. The encouraging bit: He could manage not to say or do anything foolish or rash for one more pathetic week. Then Mia would be gone and he and his life could get back to normal. The despairing part: Mia would be gone. Somehow, despite his best intentions to keep her out of his head and the regular lies he fed himself about having his feelings under control, he couldn't fool himself entirely. He was going to miss her like the dickens when she left. Like the dickens—now there was a phrase that would trigger her wild laughter, except that he wasn't going to share these current thoughts with her. Doing so would fall into the "anything foolish" category that he was trying to avoid.

During the measly few months he'd known her, she had become part of the rhythm of his days. Visiting her in person, thinking about her, reading her notes, responding to them—it was never-ending, but in a good way, like how he felt when he was adding to his growing wood pile, despite knowing he had enough wood for two brutal winters, let alone one, or when he was organizing the food he had stored up in his pantry and root cellar. Okay, so perhaps the feelings she evoked weren't really like that at all. It was a bad example. Still, time with her was satisfying and comforting—and fun—in ways that surprised him. Especially because less than a season ago, he would've, without question, said he'd never experience anything remotely like the emotions Mia kindled in him, ever again. Being so wrong about this defining belief really pissed him off.

A line from the letter that had been his undoing, the temptation he hadn't resisted, that made him renege on his vow to stop their note writing came back to him:

I never thought I'd be able to touch, or be touched, by someone for pleasure again—and I still don't know if I will be, but you make me want to.

Recalling the words, Gray groaned and slowed his pace. He hadn't, of course, reacted how he wanted to react. He hadn't rushed back to her cabin and let her touch him all she wanted until she was sure *what* she wanted.

All his surging physical desire and wild imaginings aside, however, he might've managed to withhold a response and adhere to his no-writing plan, except for what she'd gone on to say:

> *But what really shocks me—as in when it hits me I can hardly believe it's true—is that I never thought I'd be able to trust a stranger, someone that I hadn't known my whole life, ever again. But I'm finding that I do. I do.*
>
> *I'm not an "everything happens for a reason" kind of person. I think a lot of atrocities take place for no good reason at all—but meeting you, our becoming friends, was unexpected and feels like a blessing, something good when both of us have seen a lot of . . . hard times.*
>
> *Anyway, whatever happens, or doesn't happen between us in the future, I want you to know how grateful I am to you. Thank you, Gray.*

And Gray, feeling exactly the same, though he was loath to admit it even to himself, had taken the coward's way out. He had decided to seize each moment with Mia that he could, to treasure the luxury of having someone to really talk to again, to let himself enjoy the exquisite fantasy . . . After all, soon she would leave and he would be safe again.

He was almost at Sockeye cabin now and could see a flag of smoke waving above the clearing that he considered hers, could smell the homey scent of burning cedar. . . .

Dammit! What was wrong with him? If he was going to enjoy each moment he still had with Mia, he needed to banish all these dangerous feelings of wanting more. Enjoy *now*. Suffer *later*.

"Why so glum, chum?" The silly greeting made him jump—which was ridiculous. He should've expected Mia to appear any second like she always did whenever he neared her place.

"Hey," he replied cleverly.

She fell into an easy stride beside him, looking like a model for a Christmas in the Country ad or something, in a touchable, buff-colored suede coat with wooly cuffs and a soft raspberry scarf. Her casual beauty reminded him that she was someone who had a *look,* as evidenced by the cover art on contraband in his backpack, which he'd received in the mail, via Amazon, via Jo just today.

He was about to tell Mia he'd bought her old music, so he wouldn't feel weird about it, like he was spying, but then he glanced at her again and promptly forgot all cognizant thought. Eyes sparkling, cheeks glowing from the cold, hair spilling around her shoulders . . . It was like who Mia was, her innermost self, shone in every aspect of her physical being. She took his breath away—dammit! He knew it was a mistake to come see her today. Their lessons were officially finished the last time they saw each other. He should've said his good-bye then and left it at that.

Mia stopped walking abruptly and shot him a stern look. "Fess up, Gray. Tell me what's wrong—and don't say 'nothing.' I'm not an idiot. If looks could kill, the whole forest would be a black ash mess."

"I think that's a bit of an exaggeration," he said dryly.

Both her eyebrows lifted and her eyes widened comically. "Nuh—uhhh."

He shook his head.

"Seriously," she insisted, but resumed walking. "What is it?"

He sighed heavily. "I guess it's hit me that you're leaving soon and I'm kind of out of sorts about it."

"Really?" The surprise in her voice was authentic. "You're going to miss me?"

Gray literally grunted—and could've kicked himself for doing so. "Yeah," he admitted grudgingly. "And let's not pretend you didn't know it on some level."

Mia's mouth opened, then shut again. She looked pensive.

"What is it?" he asked. "What's wrong?"

"Nothing. But we need to talk."

Apparently "need to talk" also meant "in the cabin, and not until we both have a warm drink in hand." Mia barely said two words to him until they were both in Sockeye, and his outer layer of clothing was hanging by the heater. She made them something called "Ski

Jumps"—rich hot chocolate with generous dollops of peppermint schnapps and Irish Cream, topped with whipping cream. Gray stirred his with the chocolate covered peppermint stick she handed him, and a feeling of complete contentment flooded through him. He liked how she was always feeding him. "You must burn like 10 000 calories a day," she'd once said in a jokingly accusatory tone.

She settled on the couch with her own mug, sitting near him—he was always so aware of her physical presence—but not quite touching. He recalled, as he often did, the light joy her tentative high five had kindled within him. How the pressure of her palm against his had been as erotic as any skin to skin contact could be—maybe more so because it had been so unexpected and carried so much unspoken significance. Oddly, when he thought about touching her, that was the instance he usually focused on—not all their close contact while he tried to hold her down and she fought to get away. Or maybe it wasn't odd at all. One was personal, meant something, was a connection. The other was business. They hadn't had any physical contact of a personal nature since that first time—no doubt because of his outburst about rules. He was glad about it, even while it drove him crazy.

In the cozy, snug surroundings, with the flickering natural gas fireplace and Mia's warm, easy company, Gray believed in heaven. Or, heaven's waiting room anyway. If it were actually heaven, Mia wouldn't be fully clothed and she definitely wouldn't be so far away from him on the couch. He tried to stop the fantasy there.

She smiled at him and his imagination lit up again. He wished he was a stronger man, or a weaker one—whichever one would have the ability to throw caution and sense to the wind and reach out to her.

"I'd say I'm sorry our workouts are over, but it's nice to not be freezing my ass off trying to beat yours."

Gray laughed. "Yeah, I'll bet. And anyway, you're all good—strong and smart. Practice once in a while and you'll be golden."

"Jo said she'll let me practice on her."

Gray nodded.

"And that Callum will too. If I want."

Deep satisfaction made Gray nod again. He'd helped Mia arrive at this place of confidence. She would go from here and thrive. That knowledge made every bit of his personal shake up well worth it.

A tiny bit of whipping cream frosted Mia's lip. For a second all Gray could see was that line of sweetness, and he was slammed by an almost overwhelming desire to pull her close and kiss it off.

Mia gave him a questioning look that he badly wanted to answer—with action. A familiar angst filled him. He yanked a clean handkerchief out of his pocket and passed it to her.

"Your mouth has stuff on it," he said tersely.

She raised her eyebrows at his tone but took the

cloth and wiped her face. She was just as tempting without whipping cream, unfortunately—but thankfully she distracted him by shaking her head in disbelief. "I can't believe you carry a handkerchief."

"Why not? They're practical."

Her eyes crinkled in humor. "I guess. But anyway, I'm thinking about it . . . practicing with Callum, I mean. I think I'm up for it."

"You've come a long way in a short time. I guess it shows that you were right in coming here, that you were ready."

"Yeah." Mia stirred her drink with her melting mint stick. "It kind of reminds me of learning to play guitar."

"Really? How?"

"When I was a kid I remember getting so frustrated, trying and trying to get the fingering right for some song or another, and just . . . failing miserably. If I kept at it, though—kept showing up and doing the work every day, all of sudden, without warning, I'd turn a corner and just . . . have it. It caught me by surprise every time—that something so difficult, so painful, so *impossible* would suddenly be second nature. Easy. Like I'd known how all along."

She sipped her cocoa. "That's sort of how I feel about a lot of my, I don't know, *issues*. Like maybe I've mastered some of the worst of them." She smiled wryly. "Who knows? Maybe I'll even get to live like a real person again."

"You've always lived like a real person. 'Real' people live all sorts of ways."

Was it his imagination or was her reply slow to come?

"True," she said eventually. "Very true."

Mia's comparison of her time at River's Sigh to playing guitar made Gray notice something else. The cabin had guitars, at least three of them, and piles of notebooks lying everywhere.

"Are you playing again?" he asked cautiously, not wanting to poke a bruise.

"Not only that," she exclaim-whispered, leaning in conspiratorially, "I'm writing again too."

"Wow, that's great. I'm really glad for you." And he was, sincerely—but he knew his words sounded hollow and inadequate somehow.

He guessed it made sense that she'd keep pushing right until her last day, given her reason for coming to River's Sigh, but still . . . "Seems like a lot to have on the go, considering it's your last week here."

"Um, yeah, about that . . . " Mia rotated on the couch, tucking her legs up, so that she sat cross-legged facing him. "It's actually not my last week. I'm staying."

Gray almost spat out the sweet mouthful he'd been enjoying—and that now tasted like poison. "Wh— what?" he sputtered once he managed to swallow.

"I'm not leaving in a week." Mia wrapped her hands around her mug as if for warmth, although the cabin was plenty warm. Swelteringly warm, in fact. Too, too, too warm. When he didn't say anything else, she continued, "I'm buying a small business here. Relocating—well, for a year anyway. Then if I don't like it or it doesn't work out . . ." She shrugged. "I'll move somewhere else?" The last sentence came out more like a question than a statement.

Gray tried to formulate some sort of response, but his heart was racing and seemed to have lodged in this throat. He could say nothing.

Mia set her mug down, concern wrinkling her brow and pinching her mouth. "And so," she said tentatively, then made jazz hands and flashed a smile, "Good news, right? Ta-da! You won't have to miss me. We can still be friends."

"No," Gray said without hesitation. No stutter. No pause. No heart in his throat. Only anger and a sad futile whisper in his consciousness, *but what if . . .*

Except there was no what if. He wouldn't, couldn't, risk such pain again. Celine. Simon. Kip—Tracy's hollow-eyed, grief ravaged face filled his mind. Love was for the young, the strong, the optimistic . . . he was none of those things anymore. Why did Mia have to push, intentionally or not? Why couldn't they just . . . enjoy what was and not have to think about anything else? Maybe in his heart of hearts he'd fantasized about keeping their letter writing habit when she was safely . . . away. He had tried to buy the same line she was selling herself—that they were merely friends. But if she stayed? He wouldn't be strong enough.

"No!" he repeated, bolting to his feet. Mia stood too, still looking concerned, but also confused.

"What do you mean *no*?" Her head tilted as if even her physical body echoed her question.

"I told you . . ." Pain cramped through him. "I told you we couldn't *be* anything."

"Wait, *wait*. I'm sorry. I wasn't clear. I'm not asking for anything more. I like what we have. You were right. We're good like this. Safe like this."

He gaped at her. Was she actually serious? Did she really not feel it? They were the furthest thing from good the way they were. The furthest thing from *safe*.

"I admit I was worried you might not take the news well. I know you've been counting down days until I leave."

He didn't deny it, and Mia's face turned a dull, flat red—very different from the happy, light-hearted glow she usually emitted around him.

"But then, just now, today, you said you'd miss me." Her voice lowered to a whisper. "So I thought maybe you'd be happy. Happy for me, that I'm doing better. Happy for . . . us—that we're friends and will still get to see each other."

"Shit, Mia . . . I am happy for you. And you're doing better than 'better.' You're doing great. But as for the rest? You relocating, us . . ." He waved his hand, suggesting everything and nothing in one gesture, then shrugged. "It's a no. I came here today, out of sorts because it was time to say goodbye—but it is time. And whether you're living here or not doesn't change that."

Mia swallowed and her eyes no longer merely sparkled. Wet with unshed tears, they shone like moonlit pools.

Gray shrugged. "I'm . . . sorry."

"No," Mia said. "I am. You were very clear, always have been. And—oh my God," her voice rose slightly hysterically. "I hope you don't think I'm trying to force my company on you—"

Gray wished the ground could swallow him up. What a waste of skin he was. That his weakness would cause kind, funny, generous Mia pain—would make her insecure about reaching out? He made himself sick. Another wave of anger assaulted him. He forced himself to inhale deeply, then to breath out slowly.

"Of course I don't think that. What does Sam call me? The crazy recluse in the woods? The broken-down loser? Well, she's right and you should listen to her. None of this is on you—and I'm sorry you had to meet me and that I ever somehow gave you the idea I could be something I'm not."

It wasn't the good-bye Gray had envisioned, the one where he thanked Mia for putting music and laughter back into his life, however briefly. The one where he might have even let himself kiss her just once . . . to say good-bye and to have something to store in the cave of his brain, alongside the other memories of her . . . but also to try to express that maybe, if life had been different, he would've, they could've . . .

But in some ways, or maybe in *all ways*, this farewell, painful and awkward as it was, was better.

Mia nodded wordlessly, and equally silent, he geared up and hit the trail. There was nothing left to say.

Gray went straight to bed when he got back to his cabin, insulating himself from the wind that howled and shrieked through the trees and slammed against his well-chinked walls. He needed a break from his plaguing thoughts of Mia and the uncomfortable tendrils of possibility she had—quite unintentionally— sent bursting through him, finding every crack, looking for any opportunity to take root and grow. He had to blot out the memory of her hurt expression with sleep. *He had to*.

Instead of relaxing into the peaceful oblivion of nothingness, however, he dreamed it was a regular work day in his life before. He was eating a thick slice of well-buttered raisin toast and drinking coffee. Outside, dawn had yet to break and the windows facing the quiet cul-de-sac were black and rain streaked. Simon was still in bed asleep, but Celine, as was her habit, had gotten up to have breakfast with Gray. Her sleep-creased face was doughy and her hair was a bird's nest—but some deep part of Gray must've known, even as he fought to savor each detail, that it was just a dream because he had never thought she looked so beautiful. He was desperate to stay there, to not let the moment end.

He caught Celine's arm as she walked past him to get a coffee and pulled her onto his lap, then leaned his chin against her shoulder. The cozy weight of her and the soft fleece of the shapeless pink bathrobe she refused to part with was so familiar, so real, that his throat ached.

His voice was light, however—*happy* even—when he whispered, "I could stay home today. We could . . . you know."

Celine pulled away, laughing. "Nice try, silly man, but not on your life. We've got things to do, places to see."

Gray stood too. "I'm serious. I have a ton of sick days. I'll take one."

Celine's voice was fond, but no nonsense. "I'm serious too." She gave him a gentle push. "It's time for you to get a move on. Get going—and shut the door behind you."

Gray resisted, but Celine repeated herself. "Shut the door behind you! Shut the door behind you. Shut the—" Suddenly her voice was lost.

Wind roared in Gray's ears and the hammering sound of a door banging back and forth in a storm assaulted him.

Gray bolted upright, sweating profusely, but shaky

with cold. All was silent and sealed tight. Wolf lumbered up from his place by the stove and padded over to Gray's bed. Then he leaned his big head near as if to check on him. Gray patted his dog's silver fur, which glowed a coppery orange in the fiery glare coming from the woodstove's glass front. Eventually Gray rolled over and realized, narrow as his bed was, he had remained on his side. He reached out and rested his arm on the empty place. Uneasy, woe-filled sleep claimed him once more.

Gray awoke to heavy snow.

Chapter 20

SITTING BY ONE OF THE dining hall's floor to ceiling windows, Mia sipped coffee and watched huge feathery snowflakes slowly turn the world white. When she called Sam earlier, she'd been thrilled to discover Sam was free all day and totally game to hang out. They'd enjoyed a leisurely breakfast in River's Sigh's dining hall, and Jo joined them for a long while before getting back to work.

Now, however, her delight with Sam's company had turned to discomfort, and she felt like the worst kind of snoop as Sam clicked away on her laptop, trying various search terms. Gray's sad eyes and angry, tortured expression had haunted Mia since she'd last seen him and had driven her to this—finally agreeing with Sam that knowing what had happened to him would be better than not knowing. Over the months she and Gray had been meeting, Mia had flattered herself with the notion that she was helping him as much as he was helping her, but after their last visit she knew better. The words repeated in her head: *their last visit.*

She knew her feelings for him were stupid—and maybe even a sign she wasn't doing as well as she hoped. Wasn't being infatuated with someone who was fully and completely unavailable just another way to avoid having to tackle any possibility of a real relationship? But she couldn't help herself. She was drawn to him, regardless of her damage—and his. It seemed terribly unjust that they only met after life dealt blows guaranteed to alienate them from each other.

"Bingo!" Sam's exclamation made Mia jump.

Her uneasiness increased as Sam pushed her laptop closer. "This is one of those True Crime report sites, so its tone's a bit sensational, but its facts are right."

Mia reluctantly perused the article Sam had tracked down.

Constable Gray Edward Robertson was halfway out the door of his quiet suburban home in Langley, BC, about to join his wife Celine Simone Robertson and six-year-old son Simon, who were already waiting for him in their Honda Civic, eagerly anticipating a family movie night at a local theatre. Then he heard their family landline ring and turned back to answer.

Robertson didn't get to the phone, however. Instead he was thrown off his feet by a blast so powerful it propelled his family's small sedan through the wall of their carport, sending burning debris and pieces of metal flying into the air and landing blocks away.

The decorated officer and stunned father of one staggered through the massive hole in his garage into his backyard in time to see his vehicle burst into flames.

Desperate to save his wife and son from being burned alive, Robertson ran to the burning vehicle but failed to successfully pull either loved one from the blaze.

Investigators discovered a homemade bomb planted beneath the car, consisting of a metal pipe stuffed with ball bearings and ammunition, which they believe was triggered by a remote control.

Robertson, who sustained career-ending injuries in the rescue attempt, will be "badly missed" according to department chief, Ralph Edgaris. Fellow officers also mourn his loss, calling him "a second to none police officer, who loved his wife and son above all else" and "a truly compassionate guy." Robertson himself is unavailable for comment.

Mia was nauseas with grief. Poor Gray.

The article went on to identify the man behind the brutal attack as one Raymond Howard, who was 51 years old and well known to the police. Gray had testified against him in family court. Howard apparently had a long history of charges that had been dropped due to "mental incompetence." There was another lengthy paragraph citing a lack of adequate mental health resources and commenting on the complex issues surrounding people who are suffering mental illness.

Swallowing against the awfulness of it all, Mia took in the article's closing lines.

Shortly after the explosion, officers were dispatched to Howard's townhouse in a nearby subdivision. After refusing to exit for more than an hour, at approximately 9:35 p.m., Howard fled his home, fired multiple rounds from a hunting rifle, then retreated back inside.

When neighbours were cleared from surrounding housing units, a SWAT team entered Howard's residence, where he was found deceased. According to RCMP spokesperson Marie Cleric preliminary autopsy results indicate cause of death as being a self-inflicted gunshot wound.

Mia shut her eyes. How random and cruel. And meaningless. So utterly and tragically meaningless. No wonder Gray had retreated to a world for one. He'd spent his days striving to protect others from crime and violence, only to lose the people he loved most in the world in the most horrific of ways.

Eventually, she turned to Sam, still without words.

Sam's voice was uncharacteristically soft. "I didn't know what, if anything, you knew about Gray's story. I thought it might make a difference."

"I don't understand. Make a difference how? I already knew he'd lost his family and his job. I just didn't know details." Mia fiddled with her now empty mug in agitation, then shoved it away.

"I've known Gray, or, rather, have known *of* Gray, for years, but in all that time, I've never known him to have any close friends, let alone to crawl out of the bush to actively pursue a friendship or invite someone to his home."

"What about Jo and Callum?"

Sam steepled her fingers, looking thoughtful. "True, his visits to Jo and Callum have increased slowly over the past year or so. Maybe he was finally starting to heal up a bit, even before he met you."

Mia narrowed her eyes. "Look, I have no clue what you're getting at and being subtle doesn't suit you, so spill it."

Sam blinked, then laughed. "Okay, bossy pants. You got me. What I want to know is when you're going to stop mooning over Gray and jump him already?"

Jump him already? There was no way for Sam to know its history—and thus avoid—that chord-striking phrase, but the words reverberated in the tender places in Mia's psyche nonetheless. *Why don't you jump me already, you little slut? You know you want to.* It had been one of the mildest forms of abuse Ryland had sent her over and over again—ironically talking about himself, though she hadn't known it, of course.

"I'm not going to . . . what you said, ever." Mia

tried to swallow down the disgust that was rising through her like a physical thing.

Sam looked bewildered. Then troubled. Then apologetic. "I'm sorry. That was crass. I just meant . . . I think maybe you guys have something."

Mia shook her head. "You thought wrong."

"Oh," said Sam. She sounded sad—and it angered Mia.

"*Oh* what?"

Sam didn't say anything.

"Come on, out with it. I know you want to say something—that you think you know something."

Sam shook her head. "I don't know anything. I just understood something I didn't before."

"Oh yeah? And what's that, great wise one?"

Sam's eyes hardened, but she didn't take the bait— or at least not with any heat. "Some things go too deep."

Some things go too deep. Like she was too damaged and could never be whole again? Even if it were true, how dare Sam think she was so almighty and all-seeing as to make that call? How dare—

Sam held up a hand. "Whatever rage you're brewing? Put it in a song and spare me—but I do have one question. If I'm wrong, if it's not old wounds keeping you guys apart, what is it? If you sincerely aren't interested, fine. But if you are and you both let your pasts keep you from going for it . . . well, you suck."

Mia grabbed the coffee decanter and refilled her

mug. "Tell me how you really feel, why don't you?"

"Oh, don't take it so hard. That's the price you pay for being my honorary sister."

Jo returned at that moment and overheard the end of Sam's comment. She sank into a chair beside Mia. "Oh, no," she groaned. "What has she said or done now?"

"Nothing important at all," Mia said.

Sam rolled her eyes, and it made Mia smile the tiniest bit, despite herself. "But for the record, even if I was ever remotely interested in more than friendship with Gray, and decided not to chicken out, it's not in the cards. He doesn't want more—for whatever reason—and that's totally his personal business. Not yours or mine."

Sam sniffed.

"Wow." Jo glanced from Sam to Mia. "I really did miss something."

Sam shrugged. Mia shook her head. "Nothing that talking about will fix, so let's skip it and discuss something else."

"Like your new business?" Sam raised her coffee cup in a toast when Mia nodded.

"Hear, hear!" Jo lifted her mug too. "Sam's hinted at your exciting news, but as ever, despite all her big talk, she's close-mouthed about any real details."

Mia forced away all thoughts of Gray and let happy excitement in. "Well," she began, "it all kind of snowballed when I saw the cutest little shop for sale in town. . . ."

Chapter 21

THE CHANGES IN THE LANDSCAPE were impossible for Mia to get her head around. In a mere week, the greens, blues, golds and reds that made up fall at River's Sigh had disappeared. All color was so thoroughly erased it was like recalling a lovely dream or fantasy, not a memory of reality. Her new world was monochrome: unyielding stretches of snow, marred only by leafless, skeletal deciduous trees and conifers so dark and gloomy they appeared black. Dawn was indistinguishable from midday which became evening without any discernible difference in the quality of light.

A few weeks earlier, Mia started the regular habit of eating breakfast with whatever guests were staying at River's Sigh—and boy was she glad for the company now, especially with the weather making her stir crazy and slightly claustrophobic.

"It won't always be so dismal," Jo said over waffles in the big dining hall on yet another day of heavy snow. "You'll get used to it, for one. And there will be sunny winter days too, though it might be hard to believe right now. Also, Callum and I have been stringing lights all week. River's Sigh will be a wonderland again soon, you'll see."

"I have absolutely no doubt," Mia said, forcing a smile she didn't feel. All she could think about was how insular and isolated from the rest of the world the place felt, cut off by snow that made everywhere except snow-blown paths and plowed parking areas inhospitable and impassable. And it was barely December. What would it be like in January?

You're not worried about January, her inner self corrected snidely. You're worried about Gray.

And she was. Why deny it? All her thoughts were full of him—and his cabin was no longer cozy in her mind. It was more like a prison. How many months would he go without hot chocolate in the company of a friend? How long would he exist without talking to anyone?

"Mia?" Jo asked. "What do you think?"

"Pardon? Sorry, I didn't catch what you said."

Jo's brow furrowed but she didn't get a chance to repeat herself. Sam burst in on the arm of a handsome man in a huggable oatmeal sweater, which Mia instantly coveted—the sweater, not the man. Although the way he looked at Sam did cause a pang. She had imagined Gray sometimes looked at her that way.

"Mia, this is my husband Charlie—see, I told you he was real."

Mia grinned and was about to say hello, but Sam

waved her silent. "Charlie, this is Mia, the friend I told about. I'd spend more time on introductions and small talk, but we have an emergency."

Charlie didn't appear panicked in the slightest. Jo jumped to her feet, however, and Mia felt a trickle of worry too.

"What is it?" Jo asked.

"Our band canceled," Sam wailed. "Their lead singer broke his foot or something and needs surgery in Vancouver. Klutz."

"Sam is very sympathetic, of course," Charlie added, smiling.

"Of course, I am. For *us*," Sam emphasized, but a twinkle in her eye suggested her extreme diva mode was mostly put on. She sobered. "But seriously, Jo. We've already advertised that River's Sigh's big Christmas shindig is going to have live music."

Jo frowned. "Even getting a DJ on such short notice will be super tough. Every business and their dog has a party this time of year. Maybe we should lower the ticket price or refund—"

"Don't be silly," Mia blurted, and a river of shock streamed through her at the next words out of her mouth. "You have a singer right here. Ask the band if I can fill in."

Sam, Jo, and Charlie all gaped at her in total and complete silence, which made two things obvious to Mia. One, Sam must've spilled all the dirt about Mia's various issues to him, and two, they didn't realize she was—Ta-da!— much better. Or so she hoped, anyway.

Jo recovered first. "Are you sure? I mean—" She darted a quick glance at her sister, as if confirming some secret fact, but Sam's face was unreadable. "I thought you hadn't played or sang in, well, a long time."

"Sam had old information, actually."

Sam winced. "I wasn't gossiping, I—"

"Whatever you said, it's fine. I should've told you guys the good news when we talked about the shop. I've not only started playing again for my own enjoyment and sanity, I'm even—ah—" No, it wasn't time to talk about her writing. She wasn't that cured yet. "They're just a cover band, right? I can do covers. It'll be fun."

Charlie nodded, but both Sam and Jo's friendly faces wore matching looks of concerned skepticism.

"Seriously, it'll be great, and actually, you'll be doing me a favor, putting me in touch with people with musical connections in the community. After all, I'm going to need someone to buy instruments, use the recording studio, and help promote my music lessons."

As she talked, Sam and Jo's obvious nervousness on her behalf softened into something close to delight.

"Besides, if I'm going to freeze up and have another breakdown or something that forces me into complete privacy again, I'd rather do it when it's your party at stake, not once I've started a business."

Jo's mouth fell open in dismayed protest, but Sam

started laughing. "Okay, it looks like we have a singer—and it's Mia Clark. We should up the ticket prices."

They decided, of course, not to inflate the cost of admission, and at Mia's request, they agreed not to drop her name into any of the advertising, but to focus on the band alone.

Sam made it clear she thought Mia's hiding her identity was a terrible business move—that she should "capitalize" on being Mia Clark, which just made Mia laugh. "Don't worry, I'm not planning to hide it or deny it anymore, but in reality, I'm no longer that old Mia anyway. Whatever my new business is going to end up being, it will evolve naturally."

Both Jo and Charlie nodded with understanding; Sam rolled her eyes. "Natural, smatural. Letting things evolve on their own is highly overrated if you ask me."

"I didn't," Mia quipped.

"Touché," said Sam.

Jo laughed and laughed.

Chapter 22

MIA'S NERVES JINGLED AND JANGLED enough to compete with any Christmas carol as she made her way to the stage Callum and his brother Brian had constructed at the edge of a huge clearing behind River's Sigh B & B's big dining hall. The rest of the band would join her shortly and they'd check their set and do a sound test, but for now she was alone.

She climbed the stairs and took center stage. None of the main spotlights were on yet, but the trees encircling the clearing glowed with twinkling white lights. The smooth white earth—snow-blown to create a dance floor—sparkled. Colorful strobes danced and pulsed. It was a wintery disco delight, and Mia hoped desperately that she'd add to the fun, not detract from it.

Laughter and chatter from wining and dining guests carried in the night air from the direction of the hall, but Mia was almost oblivious to it. She stared out into the imagined crowd.

Why had she volunteered to fill in for the injured lead singer? Had she completely lost her mind? It wasn't performance anxiety that plagued her, however. Even though they'd only practiced together three times, she and the band clicked. It would be a good show. No, what she couldn't believe was that she was putting herself in the spotlight again, period.

What if she couldn't handle the memories it brought up? What if she had a total freak out? She'd joked about the possibility to Sam and Jo, being purposely cavalier to set their minds at ease—but it was a legitimate concern. What if someone didn't like her—or, worse, liked her too much? She had promised herself she could spend the rest of her life living invisibly if that's what she needed. . . .

The thought came swift and certain: But that's *not* what you need. And not what you want.

Her blood buzzed hot and itchy beneath her skin, a high octane mix of excitement and dread. "You can do this," she muttered. "You can. It will even be fun."

She wasn't sure the last part of her statement was remotely true, but then again, whether it was fun or not didn't matter. If she could do this, it would prove buying the shop wasn't a mistake, would show she really was ready to do things in the public eye again. The naysaying part of her brain that kept shooting darts of indecision and self-doubt would have to shut up. For good.

She visualized herself as a sound board, a trick her mom suggested when she was a shy kid just starting out that she'd held onto because it was silly and made her happy. She adjusted her nerves down, cranked her energy up—and felt it working. She was pumped! Couldn't wait for the band to hurry up and get out there too! She grabbed a mic stand and waltzed it close in an exaggerated manner, then crooned, "Yep, all the inner critics can shut the hell up."

The mic was turned off and she had whispered. No one further than a few feet away could've possibly heard her—but to her huge dismay and a massive spike in blood pressure, someone let out a low catcall, then clapped, three times, very slowly.

Mia's skin crawled, and some detached part of her observed that it was awful how even something as innocent as applause could sound sinister.

"Well, well," a smarmy male voice oozed from the shadows, "I heard the rumor, but I can't believe it's true. Mia Clark in Greenridge, BC of all places."

Mia had known her presence would get out eventually, especially once she said she'd sing. She'd asked the band to not make a big deal out of it, but she hadn't sworn them to secrecy about her identity because that would be . . . weird. And yeah, it was a semi-private party and Jo and Callum knew most of the guests—but it was still a ticketed event. It's not like they turned anybody away until it was full.

She let the mic stand rock back into place. The happy energy fueling her mood turned to sludge. She was imagining the creep factor, adding something oily and off putting to the spectator's presence because of her history. She was damaged. Paranoid. A walking mental case—

Except, wait. No. She didn't owe anyone anything. Not a civil reply. Not the benefit of the doubt. Nothing.

"So how about it? Can I have a little private pre-show, Mia?" The man's face was difficult to make out because the lights were behind him, his features in darkness. Again, something that could be unintentional and innocent . . . or not. The way he used her name, though, insinuating they had some sort of relationship when they definitely didn't, made Mia's jerk radar ping.

Mia knew she could run. She was confident he'd get nowhere near her. She also knew that a scream or yell would draw help immediately. But she suddenly found herself the furthest thing from intimidated.

"I have no idea who you are," she said calmly, "but consider this a lesson in social etiquette. It's inappropriate—and super creepy—to sneak up on someone you don't know in the dark."

The man moved forward. His oily voice hardened into tar. "I'm just being friendly. You don't have to be rude."

Just being *friendly*, hey? Some people really had no clue. Mia stared down at the guy, who was less than five feet from the stage now and fully visible. Thick and bulldoggish, his belligerent expression said he felt entitled to say whatever he wanted—and that she should like it.

Her mom's voice whispered in her ear, "It wouldn't kill you to smile and play nice, sweetie. He's just a fan, and fans are your bread and butter."

Mia suspected the man wasn't actually a threat, was just an ass. It was good practice though. She glanced down at her purple boots for a moment, then looked him square in the face. "Here's the thing. It's not rude for *me*, a total stranger to you, to not appreciate being followed outside. And even if I had been rude? Oh well."

The muffled thump-thump of feet jogging across packed snow interrupted them before the man could respond, but his scowl said tons.

Will, the band's drummer, appeared in the clearing with Lianna, the bass player, on his heels. "Scott will be right—" Will called, then stopped mid-sentence, taking in the man's posture. "Is everything okay here?"

"Yep, all's great, no worries." Mia turned, just slightly, but in a way that made it obvious her conversation with the stranger was completed. "I was starting to wonder if you slackers were ever going to get here." She played an air guitar and did her best 80s metal rocker impersonation. "Are you ready to rooooock?"

Will and Lianna laughed. "No wonder you fit in so well," Lianna said. "You're as cheesy as Will."

"What's wrong with that?" Will took the stairs in a single leap and joined Mia on stage. "Cheese is *delightful*."

The rest of the band arrived, and Mia helped finish

setting up, enjoying their silly banter and mounting energy immensely. The stranger who'd made her uncomfortable became just one more person in the crowd flowing from the dining hall, and she didn't waste another thought on him.

The gig wasn't just fun; it was a total blast.

Chapter 23

AFTER THE BIG PARTY, THE rest of December slid into January, and January glided away in one big blur.

Mia kept herself busy with Christmas celebrations, which included a week's visit to her mom's. Then she worked systematically on details related to her new business, cleaning, repainting, counting inventory, and finding suppliers for new stock she wanted to carry. She was targeting an early March opening, which would coincide with the end of her stay at River's Sigh and her move into town. And amidst it all, she played and played and played until she figured she was close to the level she'd been before she stopped.

She was grateful for the new lease on life, for her growing circle of trustworthy friends, and for little Sockeye cabin in the woods, all of which had facilitated such huge changes for her. But try as she might to forget him, Gray was never far from her thoughts.

Every so often—and promising herself each time that it was the last—she hiked the snowy trail she'd broken and maintained to the Secret Keeper just in case . . . and was disappointed every time. Not even a

Christmas card. And no telltale tracks in any direction suggesting that maybe Gray had been checking to see if she'd left anything either.

Despite having a collection of jotted tidbits and notes that Mia knew full well she'd intended for Gray's eyes, she refrained from stashing anything for him in the tree during her hopeful visits. She would, however regretfully, respect his very clear wishes.

On the first of February, early in the evening, Mia was chopping vegetables for a stir-fry when the moon, huge and luminous, rose into view over the mountains framed by her kitchen window. She put her dinner prep on hold and went out to the deck with a blanket to watch it, then thought of Gray and one of her first ever notes to him. Was he watching the moon right now too and thinking of her? Or had he happily and easily purged himself of any remembrance of their time together or their friendship? Both ideas—that he might be sitting in his isolated cabin feeling lonely, or that he might be fully satisfied by his solitary life in the wilderness—made her so sad that for once, she didn't busy herself with plans or work or writing. She trudged back into Sockeye, left her half-prepared food on the counter where it sat, and went to bed without eating.

Chapter 24

AS IF NATURE HERSELF WAS moved by the music that Gray allowed himself to listen to for one hour a day—not wanting his small CD player to burn through all his batteries before winter ended and he could walk out of the forest to get more—the clouds danced apart and a round-bellied moon kissed the earth. Its silver light illuminated the night, temporarily chasing away the shadows he'd lived with the past long, cold, dark months. Watching it, he thought of Mia, or, more accurately, thought of her yet again.

"You got your wish, you fool," he muttered, "so I don't know what your problem is."

But that was a lie. He knew exactly what his problem was. His wish had changed. He had thought he wanted to live out his days alone in the bush, reliant on no-one—and relied upon by no-one. But then he had met Mia. And they had watched the moon together and apart.

The last song on the disc started, and Mia's low, smooth voice was wistful, almost conversational. "I should've known better—but I didn't. I should've told you—but I couldn't."

The lyrics fit the mood cast by the moon a little too well and Gray knew his face was stupidly, uselessly wet. *He* should've known better. Should've realized that separation from Mia wouldn't make things better. That if anything, it would only more intensely reveal what he'd enjoyed when they were together and what he lost when they were separated.

And now it was too late. Mia, who grew brighter and fuller every time he'd visited, was no doubt in the full swing of a busy, fulfilling life now. He, the crazy guy in the woods, would just be someone she told funny, slightly disparaging stories about with a raised eyebrow. "I made it clear that I wanted us to be something, and not only did he turn me down, he was a jerk about it."

The song finished, and the player clicked off, ending his time with the CD he'd ordered and hadn't gotten around to telling her he had. A CD for a CD player, how fitting—relics from another time, a different life. Like him.

Gray peered out his cabin's solitary window, which he'd shoveled religiously the past two months to keep cleared. The endless expanse of snow beyond his gaze was void of movement, void of life. It wasn't that there wasn't beauty in this harsh, edge of the world place. It's that without someone to share it with, the beauty didn't reach deeply into him the way it had before.

Wolf, who was still disappearing for long stretches

at a go, even during this severe winter, was home for the time being, curled into a ball by Gray's feet. Suddenly he bolted awake, one ear perked. Then he leapt to his feet and padded to the cabin's barred door, making an impatient, urgent keening sound.

"Need to pee much?" Gray asked and obligingly opened the door. Wolf bounded out—and Gray froze. Standing mere feet away from the door on the shoveled pathway, framed by the banks of snow that stood much taller than her shoulder, was a *real* wolf. Female. With beautiful long legs and soulful eyes, but a too thin frame and a coat that had seen better days. Not for the first time, Gray thought how hard winter was on wild animals, how amazing it was that they survived it.

The female kept a safe distance, but didn't take off, which surprised Gray.

Wolf let out a noise Gray had never heard from him before, a puppyish sounding yipping bark. Gray didn't speak dog that fluently, but even he understood glee when he heard it. Wolf gamboled about, bucking and twisting like he was part donkey, nodding and swinging his head, not showing even a hint of aggression—which also surprised Gray.

Then Wolf bowed and gave the female a solid nudge, which she returned none too gently, though she appeared to be smiling, much the way Wolf often did.

"Well, you old son of a gun," Gray whispered. "That's where you get off to. You've been smarter than me this whole time."

Wolf paused at the sound of Gray's voice, then took off behind his lady as she trotted away.

Gray watched the beautiful duo until they disappeared into the woods. Then he shut the door heavily, feeling every bit of his none-too-old age and his own feral longings. The sentiment made him roll his eyes. That's it. He'd officially lost it. He was jealous of a couple of canines!

Settling back into his chair with a refreshed mug of tea, Gray once again wasted time with a wish—that he had walked out when the weather was at its coldest, despite the heavy snow. That he had tried, at least, to reach their tree to leave a note for Mia . . . but the weather had been too bad, even with snowshoes. And now it wasn't cold enough. The river wouldn't be frozen enough for safe passage and the season had changed before he had a chance to fix the bridge, which he had determined did indeed need repair. It would probably support him, might even last years as it was, but he couldn't trust it fully. No, he had to face facts. By the time he was able to get back to Mia, it wouldn't be "back to Mia" at all. She'd be long gone, either living in town, running her business, or having rejoined her mom and sister.

Either way, she was lost to him—a part of the living world, while he was just . . . apart.

He'd gotten what he'd wanted and worked so hard for. He was alone.

Chapter 25

MIA STEPPED ONTO SOCKEYE'S DECK and stretched her arms up as far as she could, breathing deeply. She'd had a very productive morning and early afternoon finishing lyrics to music she'd written the previous week. It felt great to be outside in the—of all the marvelous, welcome and miraculous things—sunshine. Was spring really on its way? Say it wasn't so! There was a touch of heat to the sun now, instead of the mere chilly glare that had been its signature the past few months when it bothered to show its face at all.

A twinge of wistfulness followed those thoughts. Spring, as much as she longed for it, would also be a kind of ending this year, not just a beginning. It would be the end of her time at River's Sigh. The end of her silly, if persistent, fantasy that stupid Gray would come to his senses, realize that he loved her and couldn't live without her, and come charging out of the bush— preferably without a shirt, like the first time she'd surprised him at his cabin. (Hey, it was her fantasy. If she wanted him shirtless in early February in northern BC, so be it!)

She didn't laugh at the inner joking, however, be-cause something twanged. She wanted him to realize *that he loved her*? Did that mean she loved him? Could you love someone who didn't return the sentiment? Of course. It was the definition of unrequited. But could you love someone when you'd only known them for a couple of months? Pining for them when they were out of the picture for an equal amount of time shouldn't count—but did it? She didn't know. Not for the first time, the irony struck her. She'd made a career as a kid singing about love. How laughable. At least some of her big hits had been about love gone wrong and general angst and confusion . . . that she could honestly relate to. The other stuff? She'd had boyfriends, even a few serious ones, but considered herself too young to settle down. And then she'd met Ryland and been so badly injured. The physical damage she'd suffered proved easiest to heal. Her mental and emotional wounds lingered.

And now, despite all evidence that she'd turned an important corner mending-wise, part of her still worried she was permanently stunted. In the ways of the heart she was about as confident and wise as a fifteen-year-old. Actually, the average fifteen-year-old probably felt more equipped than she did.

She exhaled loudly and stretched downwards, plac-ing her hands flat-palmed on the deck's cold planks. This line of thinking wasn't doing her any good. She couldn't change what had or hadn't happened in the past. She could only control what she did going forward. She clearly had yearnings for connection, for a partner—even, if she was honest with herself, for a *soul mate.* And that's what Gray had felt like, with all their tough workouts, long comfy silences, and equally long, rambling conversations and note exchanges.

But Gray didn't feel the same, so where did that leave her? Should she see if she could find someone else who fit her quirks the way he did? Maybe start dating again? No. The knowledge came to her hard and sure. At least not right now. The only person she could imagine allowing anything remotely sexual with was Gray and even with him, she was terrified her fantasies only went there because it was so clearly safe—as in not happening.

So that was that. Unless she miraculously developed desire for someone other than Gray, she wouldn't subject herself or anyone else to dating. A person could—and she would—live a very full life on their own.

She grabbed her new backpack and slipped it on as was her habit these days, then stepped off the deck. Even on the trails she'd already forged, the travel was hard going. The snow was starting to melt and she broke through the hard pack every few steps. Still, the air was sweet and full of the promise of longer days and increasing light, and it was great to not be cooped up.

A good hour or so later, still enjoying her walk but

feeling like it was colder than she'd initially thought and wondering if she should've worn her winter jacket, not just a shell, she realized she'd unconsciously sought out the Secret Keeper again. She sighed heavily. She really was pathetic, but since she was there she rummaged around inside the old tree. Nothing.

She turned to head back to the cabin, but didn't feel ready to be shut in for the night yet—and Sam and Jo both had prior engagements, so she wouldn't be able to visit them the way she'd started doing most evenings now too, not just mornings.

She paused contemplatively, thumbs hooked in her backpack's straps, staring up at the sky. The soft gray was hard to read but seemed bright enough. She figured she still had time before the light disappeared. She hadn't gone further east than the Secret Keeper before—Gray's cabin was north—and the idea of exploring a bit more was exhilarating. She hadn't forgotten how the slightest noises, water dripping, branches snapping, any rustle or commotion, had unhinged her when she first arrived at River's Sigh, made her feel watched, followed, threatened. . . . Now the sounds of nature being nature felt familiar, friendly, like something she was a part of—like *home*.

Also, though she knew she'd see Sam and Jo lots, even once she'd moved into town, she probably wouldn't explore the back part of River's Sigh very much in the future. There'd be other places to see, other things to do.

Pulling her zipper higher and flipping her jacket's collar so it protected her neck better from the lowering temperature, Mia struck out again. Say what you will, she thought, walking long distances through snow is a better workout than flat out sprinting.

Noticing the snow pack was considerably shallower beyond a scrubby ridge of snow-beaten, flattened brush, Mia decided to maneuver through it, so she could walk on easier ground. Then, glancing at the sky again, she set a timer on her phone. She didn't want to get caught in the dark. After fifteen minutes, she'd start back home.

She'd gone maybe thirty paces, lost in thought, when a somehow familiar yet not instantly recognizable sound caught her attention. Her ears perked. Was it a slight rushing? A wet sound?

Mia studied the landscape. Then she spotted something and froze. A black ribbon cut through the snow, opening wider here and there—far too close for comfort. Recognition sank like a weight through her limbs. Was she really such an idiot? Had she actually climbed onto the river for *easier* walking? She shivered. No worries. She'd just turn around now and ease herself back to the brush that must've—stupid her!—marked the bank.

She took a slow step, then another. The awkwardness of her gait compared to the comfortable ease she'd moved with moments earlier would've been hilarious, except . . . what was that? A large stone sticking through a spot she'd previously stepped? The ice would be thinner around a rock, so she stepped wide to be on the safe side. There was no sharp cracking sound, just a creak so subtle she wouldn't have even noticed it except that she felt her boot sink.

She tried to shift quickly right, but miscalculated the speed and depth to which her boot sank. She staggered and the extra weight on her already downward pressing leg was too much. Her boot broke all the way through. For a second, the sensation was so unfamiliar, her brain couldn't process it. And then it did. Water so cold it didn't even feel like water, it felt like blades, cut through her submerged denim-clad leg.

She was caught in a hole in the ice on the river, one leg thigh deep, one leg still above water, angled against the snow-buried ice in a clumsy split.

Houston, we have a problem.

She wracked her brain. What was the best way to cross thin ice? Right, on her belly then, if she could manage it, so her weight was more evenly distributed. The problem was she couldn't get her leg out—and fell heavily to her butt trying to. Immediately, the weight of her sank just enough that the black water soaked the seat of her jeans. No, no, no!

She rolled to her stomach and enough water seeped above ice level that she almost floated. Evil fingers of frigid water found the vulnerable warmth of her body above her waistband, stealing her breath.

Her legs and arms already felt thick and heavy.

Fighting panic, she realized she was pointed in the opposite direction from which she'd originally come. Should she try to turn herself? Doing so, the treacherous surface beneath her groaned. She felt around with both arms, blinded with tears. The ice seemed firmer in the direction of the opposite bank. Or she prayed it was. She needed to get off the ice, out of the water. She'd figure out the best route home once she was out of the water. Still, for dangerous seconds, she lay there paralyzed, her clothing wicking up the cruel river.

You could die out here. The truth of the cold statement sliced through her fear-induced inertia. Slowly, slowly, so painfully slowly, she elbow-crawled, keeping her belly low, dragging through snow, and increasingly slushy—no. No! The river was softer suddenly and she was even more wet. Wet right through, she was sure of it. It was getting more and more difficult to command her body to crawl forward and to think clearly. But when the tinkling sound, like glass breaking, hit her senses, it registered instantly. The ice around her was shattering! She flailed wildly—and couldn't even be relieved when she realized her whole body had broken through, and yet her head was still above water. She'd made it to rocky shallows, deceptively soft-looking under a mess of ice, water and snow.

Unsteady and stumbling, Mia struggled against a current that sucked around her shins and knees, threatening to knock her down and pull her back to deeper water. The stones beneath her boots were slippery with algae or some other slimy substance—a fall waiting to happen. Finally, she managed to lumber out of the river on numb legs, her backpack like a cumbersome turtle shell. Her wet clothing stuck to her, weighing her down, and already stiffening in the plummeting temperature. She looked back. There was no way she was going to get across and back to the cabin tonight. There was a bridge, somewhere near-ish the Secret Keeper. She'd taken it the time she'd trekked through the woods and up the mountain to Gray's. So that was down river from where she was now? But the light was failing and she didn't know if she should attempt to find it.

She'd take shelter under some of the bigger trees while she could still see. Maybe she could find one or two with large enough canopies that they'd have bare earth and enough dried leaves and branches to start a fire. She trembled violently. Yes, a fire. First priority.

She yelled help once, then screamed it as loud as she could. But she was completely alone and there was no-one anywhere nearby to help her. It was smarter to conserve energy, prepare a place to hunker down, and try to get dry. She staggered up the beach and into the tree line, her battered shins breaking snow like de-tached wooden things, completely without feeling. If—no, *when*—she got a fire going, she would use her whistle and her flashlight and mirror to try to signal for help.

Chapter 26

GRAY'S HEAD JERKED UP AND he glanced away from the fishing line he was reeling in. He could've sworn he heard a human cry for help. He listened hard for a few minutes, but deep, unbroken silence met his ears. And really, what were the chances? He was literally the only person living on this side of the river for hundreds of miles.

He returned his attention to his rod and reel, planning to cast one more time, then call it a night. He had noticed the opening in the river's ice the day before, and facing another yawning afternoon, decided to try for a trout or two. When had the days out here grown so long and unfulfilling? Yeah, right. Like he didn't know exactly *when*—and like he didn't know *who* the timing coincided with.

His cast, as if fueled by his sudden flare of emotions, went wild and long—but then the current caught his lure and pulled it down. The weight of the river dragged his line, as steadily and inescapably as the pull of life on time—but then the movement changed. There was a shuddering jolt, then a tug. He jerked hard on the rod to set the hook, hoping it really was a trout, not a rock or a log that he'd stuck his lure into but good. He started reeling again.

The tension on his line suddenly went slack. Shoot, the fish had gotten away—no, wait, hold that thought. The rod bounced hard. The played-out fish was only resting, steeling itself for one more fight. Silver flashed as the fish shot through the surface. Gray took his time, reeling slowly now. He wanted to net the fish, but knew the ice wouldn't hold his weight. He'd have to get it all the way to shore first.

And then he was done reeling. The fish, still fighting, writhed on the snow in front of him. You have to admire their spirit, he thought. They never give up or quit trying to survive until they have no choice.

Gray reflected on that observation for a second—and added it to the fact that he still had plenty of stew left from the other night. Then he carefully removed the barbless hook from the trout's cheek, happy it had done no damage the creature wouldn't easily recover from. The fish rested twitchily, not wanting to die, but not necessarily happy to be alive at the moment either.

"I feel you, little buddy," Gray muttered. He kicked at the ice along the river's edge until there was a small patch of open water, then retrieved the flailing fish. The lithe body twisted and jumped from Gray's hand the second he lowered it back to the water—but then, for such a long moment that Gray feared for the worse, it floated completely motionless. It was like the poor thing was stunned and unable to figure out what to do after discovering it was still alive, not dead after all.

Suddenly, without warning, it perked up and zipped beneath the shelter of the ice. There was something inspiring in that—how the creature went from seemingly unable to recuperate to full of life and off like a shot, despite its wounds and proximity to death. Mia would've appreciated the analogy too. With that thought, the tiny flash of brightness in Gray's mind darted away just like the fish. He slid his rod apart and put it in its carrier, then started back for his cabin, figuring he'd walk the shore as long as he could before trudging uphill. And he'd better get a move on.

He'd trekked a good mile or so and was glad he'd left off fishing when he did. Even with his steady pace, he could feel the falling temperature. The flirting warmth earlier in the day had been deceiving. Night was coming fast, wrapped in its all too familiar deep chill. The sky, a quickly fading periwinkle blue, would be navy soon, then black.

Despite feeling pressed for time—he could get home in the dark, but it wasn't his preference—Gray paused and sniffed the air, not with wariness exactly, but definitely with some curiosity. Was there a taint of oily, wet wood smoke in the air? He sniffed again. Yes—and that was strange because he was a long way from where anyone with good sense would have a fire.

He was about to veer toward the trail he'd take home when a disturbance along the bank caught his eye. The snow was kicked up and looked like some-thing had been dragged through it. He scanned the broken shield of ice, alarm buzzing through him. The chewed-up area was a concern. It wasn't the smooth edged, gradually enlarging hole that forms when the weather starts to warm. Some animal had struggled there. He'd once witnessed a moose drown, not far from this very spot. It had traumatized him, even though he'd known the poor beast must've already been weakened by illness or a predator because moose were normally tough survivors. The fact hadn't been much of a consolation.

Gray examined the area once more but saw no sign of struggling wildlife. Then he caught a terrifying detail in the fading light. He looked again, sure his eyes were deceiving him. But no—

Suddenly he was running from the water's edge, calling and whistling for Wolf as he did. He was following boot tracks—boots that had emerged from the river. And if someone had been dunked in there today, they were going to need help and quick. He just hoped he wasn't too late. His breath formed white puffs in the bluing light, and he prayed the temperature wasn't already below zero.

Wolf was at his side, then rushing forth, beating Gray to the ramshackle pile of . . . what? His brain struggled to make sense of what he was seeing. Clothes, obviously wet at one time because they were now rigid as boards on top of what seemed to be a pile of leaves and tree debris at the base of a cedar. His eyes locked on a familiar raspberry scarf and his blood surged so hard within him, he was momentarily staggered by dizziness. Then his head raged in a fevered panic. Mia. Mia was here? Mia had fallen into the river somehow?

He dropped his rod and scrambled toward the terrifying heap, digging through it as fast as humanly possible. He found her hunched in the hollow of the tree's massive root system, deeply buried in leaves and pine boughs. A weak fire struggled beside her, barely giving off the smoke he had noticed earlier.

"Mia—hey," he whispered.

She jumped as if he'd yelled, then pushed away some of the leaves she'd buried herself with and squinted groggily. "Gray?"

"Yeah, it's me," he growled, surly with the relief of hearing her voice and seeing her move.

"F-finally," she said through chattering teeth, a hint of her old self in her thin voice. "What took you so long?"

He couldn't bring himself to smile even a little at her attempt at levity, though he was relieved that she was obviously conscious and alert. "How long have you been out here?" he asked, reaching for her, careful not to jostle her or rub her extremities too hard, not wanting to send potentially dangerous cold blood rushing from her arms and legs to her heart.

She was shivering hard, inadequately dressed in a

lightweight long sleeve shirt and knee socks. That was it. Socks and a shirt! He wanted to yell in fury but forced himself to be calm. She did have a toque on, that was one thing. He changed his mind about trying to move her for the moment and lowered his pack instead, then searched through it.

"My . . . my clothes got wet and it was the only thing I didn't have, extra clothes. I only had . . . had a toque and dry socks and one shirt," she stammered, obviously finding speech difficult.

"Better than nothing. And you got a fire started."

He noticed she had gathered a small pile of branches to keep the blaze—if you could call it that—going.

As if hearing his thoughts and taking offense, the smoking little mess burst into an actual flame or two. "Finally," Mia breathed. She reached for some of the smaller twigs with stiff movements and added them. Within seconds the fire brightened a bit more. There was even the odd crackle and snap. "Didn't, didn't . . . want to snuff it out. Had to wait to feed it," she whispered haltingly.

Gray nodded. "Good thinking. Smart." He found what he was looking for and wrapped the polar fleece button down around her, then wrestled a pair of sweatpants onto her. She was limp and unresisting in his arms—which made dressing her very difficult.

"Mia, you still with me?" he asked when she no longer appeared aware of his presence or actions. He yanked one of his gloves off with his teeth, and pressed two fingers to her neck, feeling for her carotid pulse. It was there—and nice and steady.

He pulled off his other glove and fumbled her hands into them.

Her teeth chattered. "Yeah, I'm here. Sorry. I'm just so tired and sooo cold. I was letting you do the work. Sorry," she repeated.

Relief burned in the back of Gray's throat. She still felt cold! That was a small mercy—but it was too early for real optimism. Even if things weren't critical yet, they very well could be and soon.

"I was going to keep slowly building the fire and wait till dark, then I'd use my flashlight and mirror and see if I could get someone's attention. I didn't want to waste my battery."

"That was good thinking too," Gray muttered but he was only half aware of what she said. His thoughts raced pell-mell, searching for—and discarding—options as they occurred to him.

His place was too far away, or too far for him to carry her anyway, and the temperature was only going to keep falling now that the sun had dropped completely from the sky. He needed to get her dry and warm—and soon. Her fire wasn't going to be hot enough or last long enough unless he could find a lot more fuel. Without a decent fire, even if he rigged a tarp, it would hard to make up the body heat lost through her exposure to the river. Another possibility trickled into his head.

There was an old trapper's cabin that snowmobilers and backcountry hikers and skiers used—and sometimes even kept partially stocked. But regardless of what goods it did or didn't store, at least it would be dry. Plus, it had an old woodstove. Its most important feature, however, was its proximity. A quarter of the distance his cabin was—and on flat terrain. That he could manage with Mia in his arms.

He spent precious minutes lowering her back to the cold earth again, stuffing her wet clothes into her backpack, and then shoving the works into his bigger one and putting it on again. Finally, he carefully wrapped her in the reflective blanket he always carried.

And then he set off, racing against the assailing cold.

In his hurry, he forgot about the stream—just one of many—that fed into the river near the derelict cabin, and he didn't see it in the darkness. Before he knew what was happening, he had plunged past his knees into cold. Somehow he managed to keep hold of Mia and by some miracle she was conscious enough to tighten her grip on his neck. By the time he lurched onto dry land again, however, he was soaked past his waist. His snow pants were so waterlogged, it was like wearing a lead suit.

His bad leg burned like it had been torn off and with every step he expected it to fail him.

But he had to be close. They had to be—

Chapter 27

A SHADOW DARKER THAN THE myriad of other lurking shadows hulked into view. For a few ragged breaths, Gray was sure it was a figment of his desperate imagination—but he pushed on, one foot in front of the other, one foot in front of the other, one foot in front of the other. The square-shaped wraith grew more distinct, gleaming dully in the scant moonlight. Four walls. A roof. Relief made him weak. They'd made it. He sagged beneath Mia's weight and kicked at the door, which was stuck in its frame, swollen stubbornly in place by time and bad weather. When it finally let loose and creaked open, they practically fell inside.

Gray set Mia, who was limp and boneless and heavy as wet cement, on the floor and struck a match. What he saw made him want to weep. A rough bed in a weathertight corner—with blankets. An ancient stove, like he'd remembered. A small stack of firewood! It didn't matter that he could feel the outside air rushing in and see the night sky through gaps around one of the windows. He could work with this.

The terror that had flooded his system and propelled him on since finding Mia by the river drained abruptly, leaving him disorientated and shaky. Gray closed his eyes and allowed his mind to go there, to ask *what if,* for one horrible minute. Then he pulled a long shuddery breath into his stress-seized lungs and got down to doing what needed to be done.

MIA'S EYES SHOT OPEN AND were met by darkness. Where was she? The dusty air was closed-up smelling and thick with smoke from a poorly vented fire, but Mia found it deeply comforting. They had shelter from the worst of the elements. She was dry—

Wait, those were weird thoughts.

Groggy snippets of memory dripped in and she shivered. The river. Her fall. Gray. An attempt to reach some dark little cabin. Apparently, they'd made it, or she had. Was Gray just a dream? Against her bare skin, musty flannel sheets had the strange soft-yet-rough texture of line dried fabric. They were warming slightly with her body heat and Mia sighed, almost unconscious with exhaustion and relief. So she wasn't actually frozen solid, it had just felt like it.

She burrowed deeper beneath the heavy weight of the top sheet and scratchy wool military blankets she thought Gray had tucked around her. Gray again. Was she delusional or had he saved her? Another full body shiver, almost a convulsion, shook her limbs and rattled her jaw. She wasn't sure what caused this tremor, however: the aftereffects of her exposure to the cold or the barrage of complicated emotions that Gray evoked.

Where was he anyway? Maybe she really had imagined him? But then how had she gotten here, wherever "here" was? Every so often she heard a scuffling bump or rustle that she'd assumed was him, but maybe it wasn't. Maybe it was a rat or a raccoon or . . . worse. Maybe he'd disappeared back into the night when she'd dozed off. Maybe he'd left once he'd gotten her to a place where she'd probably survive without his help. She wouldn't blame him. And she couldn't hear Wolf.

She opened her eyes again and scanned the deep shadows. "Gray?" The shrillness of her voice made her jump. She wouldn't have recognized it as her own. "*Gray?*"

Something heavy scraped along the rough plank floor and the hair on the back of her neck prickled.

Then a familiar low voice whispered, "Yeah?"

"*You're here.*" Her absolute relief was obvious even to her own ears.

"Yeah."

Oh, man of many words! Still, she'd never been so grateful for his monosyllable responses as she was now. "Where are you?"

"By the stove."

"Oh?"

"I've been feeling around to see if there's any

wood I missed, dry or not. The fire's pretty much out, and I don't know if it got the place any warmer."

Mia hesitated. "You can sleep up here. You *should* sleep up here. You'll freeze otherwise."

More memories trickled in. Gray carrying her. Them hitting a creek or something? He'd gotten as soaked as she was. Sitting in wet clothes all night would be miserable at best and an extreme health hazard at worst. And if he'd stripped? Well, that was a non-solution too. Even if he could get that small stove blazing, the cabin would be cold. Now that her eyes had adjusted, she could make out black sky and stars through gaps in the walls.

Another wooden creak. It was the only sound in the quiet room for a long time.

Mia slipped her hand out from under the covers and was shocked by the sharp and instant chill. Her teeth rattled with another shiver, and she patted the foam mattress. "Come on. If you catch hypothermia too, we'll both be in trouble."

"I hung our clothes by the fire to dry," he said gruffly. "I'm naked."

"Me too." She kept her voice casual, but anxiety raged through her. He wouldn't think she was inviting—

"But I guess it would be better," he said, interrupting the thoughts she hardly let herself articulate. "If it's really all right with you."

"I said so, didn't I?"

There was another long, weighty silence. Then movement in the shadows. The blankets drew back. Mia gasped as the frigid air stabbed at her finally-starting-to-warm flesh.

And then Gray's muscular legs slid behind hers and the rock-hard expanse of his chest grazed her back. Cold radiated off him in waves and she felt him shivering too. Good thing she'd thought to tell the ninny to crawl into bed with her!

The quarters weren't as close as she'd been expecting, however. He wasn't actually touching her, which seemed strange because if the homemade bunk was even as big as a modern twin sized bed, she'd be a monkey's uncle—and neither she nor Gray were small people.

Suddenly, she realized what he was doing.

"You can't hold yourself up on your arms all night. You need rest."

"We'll touch."

And here she'd always thought she was the most contact-averse person she knew. "I don't mind." To give her words clout, she rolled slightly, reaching her arm behind her and feeling around. She touched his hip—and bit her lip, grateful it was just a hip—and found his flank, then tugged at him. He capitulated to her non-verbal command and relaxed his weight onto the mattress. Mia was very aware of the fit of her butt against his pelvis, the sensation of his quads pressing into her hamstrings, and the firmness of his furry pecs against her shoulder blades. His skin was still too cold for the contact to be pleasurable, but it occurred to her that if things between them were different, and she didn't still have so much fear, this could be very erotic indeed.

There was a problem though. Her one arm was pinched beneath her body and threatening to fall asleep if she didn't move it. She wiggled her hips, trying to rest her arm under her head instead of her torso. Doing so, she unintentionally grinded closer to Gray. His skin already seemed warmer, but that wasn't the only change. He had an erection, and now it was pressed into the curve of her buttocks. She was shocked by how natural and non-threatening it felt—was happily surprised by a flooding heat deep inside her. So she didn't just find Gray attractive when there was no chance he'd come near her . . . It was an interesting and enticing revelation—as was the fact that he clearly wasn't as disinterested in her as he continually insisted.

"Sorry about that," he said dryly.

Despite the darkness and having her back to him, Mia knew exactly what expression he wore. If she rolled over quickly enough and managed to trace his mouth with a finger, she'd find the curve of his wry grin instead of the all too frequent glower.

"It's okay," she said, shocked yet again to realize it was totally true. She was feeling a lot of things, but panic and anxiety weren't on the list.

"I won't act on it or anything. Don't worry."

She wasn't worried. Not even close. But she was awash with some emotion. Not disappointment, surely? Except that's exactly what it was, tempered with relief, yes, but still . . . disappointment. Very interesting.

Gray's forearm folded over her ribcage and his hand rested securely beneath her ribs. His erection was still a . . . presence. Then he let out a soft rumbling snore that she felt against her back more than heard.

Something tight and knotted up within Mia loosened and unfurled. She was suddenly filled with a sense of rightness, a crazy release, a sweeping away of the final dregs of pain she hadn't even realized were still affecting her. It was like she'd had a vertebra out in her back for so long she'd gotten used to it, had even worked out ways to live and thrive despite it, then, unexpectedly, it had clicked back in. Her relief was more like joy. She really wasn't going to be disabled or suffer chronic pain forever.

Gray was a good man. *A safe man*. Such men really did exist, like she'd known all along, just hadn't been able to remember clearly because of the things that had been pushed out of place in her. But now . . .

She sighed and let herself sink into the delicious dreamy place you occupy just before sleep. She would not have wild sex with Gray, sadly, because he didn't like her enough—or maybe the actual problem was that he did. Either way, he didn't want a relationship because of the things that had been pushed out of place, damaged, in *him*. It was an extra loss because she finally trusted her ability to read people again and knew she couldn't do better than choosing someone like Gray. Honorable. Kind. Valiant. And oh . . . the feeling of that body of his pressed up against hers.

Chapter 28

GRAY DIDN'T SLEEP—OR NOT IN the bordering on unconscious way he would've benefited from anyway. The satin-sleek heat of Mia's curves against his increasingly warm and resurrected flesh prevented it.

She felt perfect in his arms, and the sleeping weight of her pressed against him made every part of him ache. He inhaled the fragrance that he'd come to associate as *her*—oranges and sandalwood, still lightly discernible despite the musty, cedar-smoked air. It was the scent of laughter, new memories, potential, and wall shaking sex. . . . It was excruciating.

He rubbed his eyes and felt wetness. Agony roiled through him, like he was spilling blood not tears.

Mia did not remind him of Celine. The source of his torture was not that this mermaid woman made him long afresh for what he and his much-loved wife had enjoyed. No. It was that Mia made him want new things. Different things. A future with someone that wasn't Celine—the very idea of which he had found unbearable for so long.

Getting to know Mia forced Gray to confront a fact

he had always despised and felt traitorous and guilty for. No matter how often he'd wished for it, he hadn't died when Celine and Simon did—or not all of him had. And nowadays, painful shoots of life, *of wanting to live*, sprouted with greater and greater frequency.

At first, whole hours had passed without Gray tangibly mourning Celine, then days, even weeks, once he'd started traipsing around with Mia. He had held the truth about his terrible betrayal at bay, willfully choosing denial, but he couldn't keep up the farce any longer, even with himself. He wanted Mia and, worse, he *wanted* to want her. He'd tried to resist. He'd even shut himself away all winter without her—but it hadn't helped. His thoughts were consumed by her and now here she was, snuggled up against him.

What am I supposed to do, Celine? he raged in his head. But Celine was silent, not even deigning to visit him in a dream. She was gone. And Mia. Mia was here. In flesh and in spirit, pressed up close, her heart beating in time with his.

When the earliest gloom of morning approached, transforming the darkest of the cabin's shadows to hazy apparitions, Gray did what felt like the most difficult thing he'd had to do since he buried his family. He disentangled himself from Mia's soft body and left her.

The razor sting of the air was welcome and deserved, bringing with it a cutting clarity. He lifted the melted lump of gold he wore chained around his neck—the remnant of Celine's wedding rings—and pressed his lips against it.

The woodstove's weak fire had failed to dry his clothing. He forced his aching limbs into his damp shirt and pants, pulled on his icy wool socks, and jammed his feet into his boots.

In equal silence, Wolf roused himself from sleep and followed his master out into the struggling daylight.

Chapter 29

IT WAS STRANGE HOW THE cold could be both a curse and a blessing, Gray thought. Yesterday, it was a predator, threatening their health, even Mia's life. Today it was his salvation, keeping the snow crisp and frozen, which made for easier, safer traveling than trudging through melting slop. Even with that small mercy, however, his leg was punishing him and didn't appreciate the added weight of the well-stocked pack. Getting up to his place and down again had taken longer than he'd hoped. Mia would probably be awake and panicking. He should've woken her and told her he was going, or left a note at least, so she'd know where he was, but it was too late for should haves now.

When he finally arrived back at the trapper's cabin, Gray felt nervous—and that made him even more nervous. He was used to a pummel of conflicting emotions, but *nervousness* wasn't generally one of them. He reached for the door, only to have it slam open, practically knocking him in the face.

He stepped back quickly and Mia gasped, "Oh, it's you!"

"Yeah," he said, then added, "What the heck are you wearing?"

It probably wasn't the smoothest segue into what he needed to say, but it was a fair question.

She was wrapped in wool blankets which she had belted with a sheet. What appeared to be pillows, again bound tightly with strips of sheets, adorned her feet. She glared at him. "I have no dry clothes and the ones you forgot are still wet. I was left here to walk out on my own by the man who . . . " She trailed off, as if suddenly aware that whatever she wanted to accuse him of probably wasn't fair because "the man who" was back. Her shoulders slumped.

"Hey," he said gently. She wouldn't meet his eyes and it made him feel terrible. "I'm sorry. I didn't wake you because you needed as much rest as you could get." He shook his head. "It didn't even occur to me that you might think I'd left you to fend for yourself, naked and alone in the woods, until I was already on my way back."

He shrugged out of his pack and rested it at her feet as evidence of why he'd had to go.

Mia's face showed a flicker of her usual humor and she motioned at her woolen robes. "Alone, maybe, but as you can see, I'm hardly naked."

"Yeah, I do see that—and it's a damn shame."

She started at his openly flirtatious tone and words, and Gray didn't blame her. He'd been giving her nothing but mixed signals for too long. He had to explain.

"There's something you need to know, Mia." He took a deep breath. "I am yours."

Chapter 30

MIA GAWKED AT GRAY, WHO seemed unfazed by her confusion.

Then, like he hadn't just said the most nonsensical, unclear thing in the world, he moved past her and into the cabin, which by daylight was more of an eyesore and much less the haven it had seemed the night before.

"I'm sorry. Come again?" she said, then was distracted by the things Gray pulled out of his backpack. Warm soft looking clothes—men's, but beggars couldn't be choosers. A package of crackers. A large stainless-steel thermos. Her stomach growled audibly. Gray turned, smiling. "Stew. Want some?" She did, she so did—but first she wanted, *needed*, him to clarify.

She shook her head, then nodded, then shook her head again.

Now he looked confused too.

"I do want stew, I'm starving, thank you," she exploded. "But first I need . . . you have to explain what you just said. About you being . . . " She couldn't finish her sentence. It was too embarrassing. She must've misheard or misunderstood.

He nodded like she'd actually completed the thought, then set down the thermos he'd been about to open. "I should've known better, but I didn't. I should've told you—but I couldn't."

"*What?*" Mia recognized—of all things!—the lyrics to her own song, but couldn't figure out their relevance or how he'd even come across them.

"We should eat first. Then talk. Sit down."

"Pardon me?"

"Okay, talk first. Fine."

Mia arched an eyebrow. Gray shook his head and appeared to blush behind his big beard, which was the craziest and fullest she'd ever seen it—a detail that had eluded her in the freezing daze of the past night. "Sorry, I haven't talked in a few months. I always blab too much, on and on, babbling almost incoherently, or talk too sparely to try and compensate. I'm always extra weird at first."

"And extra shaggy."

He rubbed his invisible chin and smiled. "Yeah, I guess. I don't groom it when I'm alone. No point—and it's warmer."

She didn't want to talk about Gray's beard or his being alone and she wished she hadn't accidentally changed the subject. He seemed to sense it and scratched his forehead as if searching for words.

"Okay, the thing is," he finally said, "that's the only way I can think to put it. I am yours. Two months plus, alone in a one room cabin, pretty much snowed in, gives a man a lot of thinking time—too much thinking time, maybe. And what I thought about, pretty much exclusively, is you."

Mia's sinuses burned and she blinked.

"I want to be with you in whatever way or however it works for you, but I get it if I've lost my chance, and I don't blame you if I have. Then I'll just be like Wolf. Always yours, but you won't have to see me a lot if you don't want to."

This had to be an example of his "babbling almost incoherently"—but Mia wouldn't have changed his words for anything. She sank onto one of the cabin's rough benches. "I think we might have to revisit this conversation when you're not half-bushed."

"Deal." Gray eased himself down beside her, favoring his bad leg more than usual. After a minute, he added, "But can you give me a hint about how you're leaning? Do I have a snowball's chance in hell?"

Surprise danced through her and escaped in a laugh. "I'm so sorry. I didn't think I'd have to explain. There's no chance at all."

Gray looked utterly crestfallen. Mia pressed her hand to his weather-roughened, scarred and bearded cheek, then rushed to explain. "That is to say—no chance at all that I wouldn't take you up on . . . being my Wolf."

The disappointment creasing Gray's face was instantly replaced by warm affection, but he also looked embarrassed. "Uh, yeah, okay, not my smoothest line there."

"Do you ever have 'smooth lines'?"

Gray put his hand over his heart in a parody of wounding, then grinned an unquestionably wolfish grin. "No, but I have other talents."

His meaning was abundantly clear and Mia's insides knotted with desire, not anxiety. Was he going to kiss her? And would kissing him possibly be as good as she'd blown it up to be in her imagination? She looked at her hands, clenched in her lap. Okay, so perhaps there was some anxiety, but memories of the previous night and the sensations she'd felt reassured her that when the time came, her own inner animal would take over just fine.

All joking left Gray's face. "I love you, Mia."

"*What?*"

"You heard me."

"Like in a friendly, companionable way, you mean."

Laugh lines creased Gray's eyes, but his voice was serious. "Definitely as a friend and companion, but also in every other way a man can love—or want to love—a woman." He took her hands, unclenched them, and didn't let them go.

Mia's heart and throat were momentarily too full to speak, but finally she managed. "I—I might've daydreamed about this, but now . . . well, I don't think I ever really expected it to happen. You're probably going to have to repeat yourself a few times."

Gray smiled down at her and his eyes held an age-old question. Mia's insides surged as she nodded and lifted her face to his. When he bent in slowly and pressed his mouth to hers, Mia tasted coffee and peppermint gum and it hit her: this was real, not a feverish dream or a near death reverie. Gray was kissing her. She was kissing him. And it was perfectly natural. And wonderful. And terrifying. And safe.

"Not fair," she said when they broke apart.

Gray's eyebrow quirked.

"You've already had coffee this morning!"

He laughed. "Not quite the response I was hoping to elicit."

The bubbling joy Mia felt made her a little shy, which was silly. "Oh, don't worry. That wasn't the only response. Not even close."

"Mmm, good to hear," Gray growled, "and something we'll have to explore further." His self-satisfied, flirting tone changed abruptly, however. "But yeah about the coffee. Guilty as charged. I had to eat something at my place or I wouldn't have made it back." His expression darkened. "On that note. There's something else I need to tell you, something I should've said before I started any of this today, but I was selfish."

Apprehension quaked through Mia. "What?"

"It's about your fall in the river."

"My—" Suddenly Mia understood all too well, and she couldn't fault him. He'd lost his wife and son in a monstrous event; her cavalier stupidity about the dangers of nature must seem unforgivable. Her head drooped. "I know. I was beyond foolish. I'm sorry."

He stared at her. "What? No, *I'm* sorry. It's all my fault."

"What?" she echoed, confused.

"Why are you apologizing?" he queried.

They each cracked tentative smiles. "You first," said Mia. If he wasn't angry with her, what could possibly be wrong?

"About the bridge," he began. "It's my fault you fell in. I knew one of the supports had weakened, but I thought it had time, that *I* had time." A vein was visible at his temple and his hands were balled fists. "You could've died."

She stared at him. Yes, she could've—but even if she had used the old bridge and somehow fallen off, it wouldn't have been his fault. Did he really think the safety of the whole world was his responsibility? That it was his failing if something failed? "I didn't use, or fall from, the bridge." Humiliation revved her heartbeat and made her hands tremble. She'd been so careless. So stupid. "I was out walking and it was difficult moving through the snow. Then there was this scrubby brush part, and just beyond it the way looked clearer, easier—" She trailed off, trying to read what Gray thought about her now. Would he take back all the tender things he'd said? She wouldn't blame him.

He was shaking with . . . what? Rage? Contempt? Mia couldn't tell.

"You're serious?" he roared. "You went out of your way, consciously chose to walk on the unstable, unknown river because it looked *easier*? Are you nuts? Do you know how dangerous that was? Do you have any idea how easily you could've died?"

Gray's voice grew louder with each word, each disbelieving question. Mia shrank back, heartsick. Suddenly, he stopped talking and stared into her stricken face.

"Oh no," he said. "*No*." He put his arm around her and pressed his forehead against hers. "I'm sorry for yelling. I didn't mean to scare you. Just the whole situation, how close you . . . I was terrified."

"I'm not scared—and I understand," Mia whispered back. "And *I'm* sorry. I won't blunder about without thinking again." The conversation reminded her of something else that needed to be addressed before they let their hearts go any further.

"There's another thing we need to talk about," she said.

Gray looked like he was waiting for a literal axe to fall. "What?"

"I looked up the details about how Celine and Simon . . . were killed."

Gray inhaled sharply, like she'd punched him.

"And I'm so sorry, Gray. I can't even imagine how

hard that must've been, how hard it still must be."

"Mia, I—"

"Wait, I'm not quite done. I think I get how people acting in reckless or thoughtless ways ignites panic or anger in those who love them. There are so many things we can't help or avoid, that the ones we can—"

Gray shook his head and smiled a sad smile. "It wasn't your fault, Mia. People get into trouble outdoors sometimes—and indoors. Every aspect of life has risk. Couch potatoes risk heart attacks. Hikers risk other things. And actually, you were pretty prepared. You need to carry a full set of replacement clothes, though, in the winter especially."

Mia nodded.

"But also don't take my fretting too seriously. Everything sets me off, Mia—and nothing does. I'm a lot better, but I'm still predisposed to see danger and potential trouble everywhere. I'll keep working on it."

Mia cleared her throat, feeling the pain in his eyes all the way to her heart. "But you do know that I will die sometime, right?"

Gray jerked away, so alarmed that Mia almost checked her chest to make sure her heart hadn't exploded without her knowing it. "What's wrong? Do you have some health condition?"

She shook her head. "I'm in perfect health. And I don't mean right now. I just mean, well, sometime."

"Well, of course you will. *Sometime*."

Mia shot him a look. "Yeah, but are you okay with

that? With the risk of being hurt again, I mean? I need to know you won't get all squirrely again or inform me out of the blue that we can't even talk or be friends or—" Her voice cracked with embarrassingly transparent emotion.

"I'm sorry I hurt you. I'm an idiot, and no, I won't make the same mistake again." Gray lowered his face back to hers once more. This, their second kiss, started out sweet and slow—but so quickly progressed to a body melting, lust stirring workover that Mia forgot what they were talking about until they broke apart, panting slightly, and Gray whispered raggedly, "I will not be okay with it, by the way. Not even close. But the way I see it, I only have two choices: live life, like *really* live and love you, get to have you—or squander my life, making pain and loss my only reality by losing you when I don't have to."

He kissed her again and Mia wanted to purr and rub her body up and down him. It was actually a bit embarrassing what just being near him did to her, but at least she knew with growing certainty that she'd have no problems in the physical aspects of their relationship—unless you considered never wanting to stop a problem. "But do me a favor," he whispered into her hair, interrupting her libidinous thoughts.

"Anything." She winked. "Or almost, anyway."

He didn't joke back, and his warm eyes glowed with heat and passion. "Give me fifty years. Please."

"Easy fella," Mia teased. "We just met." But inside

Mia thought, Oh, dear, sweet man, and prayed that she could honor his wish.

Gray feigned another mortally wounded look and she softened. "Fine, I'll see what I can do."

He laced his fingers through hers and pressed a kiss to her knuckles. "Good enough," he said. "I'll take it. Now let's eat some stew and get you back to River's Sigh."

"Sit," Mia grunted in agreement. "No talk. Eat. Go."

Gray's beard twitched as he grinned. "I think you need to spend more time around people, Mia. You're getting a little bushed."

Chapter 31

SINCE THE CLOSE CALL, GRAY and Mia enjoyed the bulk of every day together, though Gray spent his nights and mornings back at his place because of his chickens and Wolf—and even being apart that much was torture for him. The more time he spent with Mia, the more he wanted to spend with her. She made everything special, from watching old movies on Sockeye cabin's little TV with bowls of buttery popcorn, to continuing their workouts—focusing more on general fitness, less on being able to flee or fend someone off—to cooking meals together or reading quietly side by side in the Adirondack chairs by the fire, not speaking a word. She'd dragged him up town a couple times to go grocery shopping and he was stunned to discover that with her hand in his, even *that* was fun.

"I'm sorry I'm such a homebody," she apologized one afternoon after spending hours playing her guitar while he half snoozed, half listened on the couch, content as a cat in the sun. "I hope you don't find our days boring. We could do something more exciting . . .

if you want."

"You're apologizing to *me* for being a homebody?" He laughed. "I've never left my house—haven't wanted to—so much in years." He took her face in his hands and watched the light play in her lovely eyes for a moment, then kissed her deeply. It still blew him away that he could kiss her. Touch her. Hold her.

"Everything about you," he said a few minutes later, "about *us*, is exciting for me. Just perfect, in fact." And it was.

Today they walked along the river and found themselves on the little bridge that Gray had shored up two days after Mia's dunk. You'd think after the near brush with disaster in the same waters, they'd want to stay clear—but no, they sat on the edge of the bridge, dangling their feet in the rushing current, splashing and shrieking with laughter like teenagers.

The water was so cold that the odd chunk of ice still floated by occasionally, knocking against their legs. Their calves and shins were strawberry pink, but Gray was warm all the way through.

He'd felt intoxicated the past weeks, perpetually buzzed on the potent cocktail of early spring and the awakening—and welcoming—of long dormant desires. Each germinating hope and new root of possibility for the future added to his happy drunk, and every time he looked at Mia's flushed with laughter cheeks and shining eyes, he knew she was feeling the same. The sweet air promised new growth and blooms of every kind and they were wild with it, as if the heady saps bringing the trees and shrubs back from the brink of death to verdant life coursed through their veins too.

Gray had his arm over her shoulders and she felt so right pressed against his side that the happiness he felt was almost an ache. "This is all so . . . " He trailed off. "I don't know . . . sometimes I think I must be dreaming."

Mia shifted and pinched his forearm.

"Ow!"

"Not dreaming, I guess." She giggled.

"That's not very scientific—and there's a stiff penalty for people who pinch." He clenched his arm around her waist, holding her from getting away, then tickled the tender flesh beneath her soft jersey shirt.

"No, no." Mia squirmed, then laugh-screamed. "No! I hate being tickled. Stop it!"

Gray released her immediately. Shit, he hadn't been thinking at all.

Mia pulled her shirt down, surprised—then understanding spread across her face. "Oh Gray, no . . . I'm sorry. I was fine."

"I know some kinds of stuff, like being restrained, might bring up bad memories. I never want to . . . be a trigger."

Mia nodded. "I don't think *you* could be—maybe before but not now. And I want us to be normal, not to have to walk on eggshells. How about you just . . . be yourself and if anything ever bothers me, I'll say so. Specifically."

Gray looped his fingers through hers and rubbed her knuckles with his thumb. Normal. What did that even look like for people who'd been through the kinds of things he and Mia had experienced? He'd been so caught up in the pleasure of it, he'd almost forgotten loving someone was also a huge responsibility.

Mia was studying him, her eyes pensive. Then she shook her head lightly. "Get out of your head, Gray."

"What?"

"You're not dreaming—and we're not living nightmares anymore either." She repeated her earlier pinch, a grin curving her gorgeous mouth.

It took him a second to catch up, then he shook his head. They still had serious things to discuss and figure out—and they would. Eventually. For now, he couldn't resist her or the way she made him feel as silly and fun as she was. "What did I tell you about pinching?"

Her eyes widened and she raised her hands coyly. "I have no idea, I'm sure."

He grabbed her again and tickled her until she laughed madly—then he pulled her into his lap, so that she straddled his hips, facing him. He slid his hands up her body, cupped the lacy confines of her breasts, then undid the clasp of her bra.

When he rubbed his calloused thumbs across her erect nipples, Mia inhaled sharply—a sound that sent waves of want crashing through him. Her eyes glinted. "Is this another one of your stiff penalties?"

"You have no idea," he said—which made her laugh like he'd tickled her again.

Chapter 32

MIA WOKE EARLY ON FEBRUARY thirteenth, her thoughts a jumble. For the first time since her misadventure in the river and being rescued—and so happily surprised—by Gray, she hadn't slept well. And she knew why. Time was advancing too quickly and like it or not, changes were coming. Mia wanted to freeze the days, keep them, hold them exactly as they were. She loved everything exactly as it was, especially with Gray.

She'd given Jo notice for March first, which was good timing for them both. Jo had kindly given Mia a monthly rate over her long stay and Mia didn't want her to miss out on high season profits. And Mia was excited about the rental she'd found on the south side of Greenridge, a rustic farmhouse sitting on a secluded half acre with lots of trees. She'd have privacy, but still be only five-minutes' drive from her little studio and shop. All perks aside, however, there was no arguing that it was far from River's Sigh, which made it even further from Gray.

While they talked freely about every subject that

came up, they hadn't broached how much—or even if—they'd keep seeing each other once Mia had a life and business and commitments in town. Gray had said he was her wolf, but Mia couldn't help but notice that Wolf did his own thing, which pretty much meant he wandered the four corners of the forest, didn't spend a lot time in domesticated company, and only visited Gray when the spirit—or his appetite—moved him. Gray had said he loved her—but love meant different things to different people.

They needed to have a serious talk, not just one of their epically lovely ones where all the realities of life fell away—but she had a gig later in the day. The band she'd sang with for Jo and Callum's Christmas party had an 80s-themed show booked at one of the local pubs and she'd agreed to sing a set with them. Then tomorrow was Valentine's Day. She didn't want to spoil what should be a fun romantic day by being neurotic. . . .

By the time Gray walked into Sockeye just after noon, she practically pounced on him. "Are you sure you don't mind coming?"

He looked slightly baffled as he claimed one of the high stools by the cabin's breakfast bar. "Coming where?"

"To the pub tonight."

"Not at all. Happy to, in fact."

"And I have to go help set up and rehearse later today for a bit. The guys will pick me up." Like they had every day the past week, she thought, so why was she making it a big deal now?

Gray apparently thought she was being weird too. His brow furrowed. "Hey, come here," he said. When she didn't, he reached out and took her hand, then tugged her gently closer until she was standing nestled between his legs. "What's up?"

She didn't reply right away, and he traced the curve of her cheek and jaw with a work roughened finger. "Let's start again," he said. "Kiss me hello and then we'll solve whatever's bugging you."

If only it was that easy, Mia thought, but she couldn't help grinning and leaning in obligingly, both reveling in—and trying to curb—the crazy things being this close to Gray always did to her insides. As they kissed, Gray put his hands on her hips and pulled her closer still. She practically moaned as she felt his mutual desire pressing against her stomach. When they broke apart, Gray was rueful. "That's both better and worse," he complained.

Mia laughed and started to shift away, but Gray closed his legs, trapping her close, his gaze hot on hers. "I meant it one hundred percent when I said I'm happy to take the physical side of our relationship really slow—but I'd be lying if I didn't admit another part of me, a huge part, in fact, can't wait to take things really fast."

Mia snickered. "A huge part of you, hey? Brag much?"

Gray flushed, which made her giggle even harder—but suddenly she felt super serious and her smile fell from her face. She caressed his beard that was trimmed and groomed again, at least by bushman standards, then rested her palm on the scars that she knew were there, mostly hidden by his full beard.

"I think that's what's bothering me."

"My huge part?" Gray moved his eyebrows up and down comically, but Mia just shook head.

"What are we doing, Gray? I'll be moving into my own place soon, opening the store and working full-time, at least until I hire someone to handle the retail side of things, but—" Her voiced died when a morose, questioning look dimmed the glow in Gray's warm eyes.

"What?" she asked, alarmed. "What did I say?"

"I thought we knew what we're doing. I thought you understood that I'm yours—and I thought you wanted to be mine."

"Well, yeah, we said that and I do . . . but I need to know what that means to you. The words sound simple, but they're not. *You're mine*. What does that mean? That you'll visit me once a week? Or that we'll be part of each other's everyday life? That we'll build a home of some kind together, or—"

Gray exhaled like he'd been holding a big breath. "Oh, okay, that's better."

"What is?"

"I thought you were backing out, trying to break it

243

to me gently that you don't want me the way I want you—"

"No, I think maybe I want you *too* much, like more than you want me. I don't want to see you once or twice in a blue moon and know you're lonely and squatting on some mountain the rest of the time."

Gray put his finger over her mouth. "One. I'm not squatting exactly. I own a thousand acres of backcountry. I didn't want to do all the work and shell out all the money to get myself settled off the grid, only to have some government official decide they wanted to clear cut it. This way I can never be booted off and if I ever leave it, it'll be like a small nature sanctuary."

Mia's breath hitched at his "*if* I ever leave it" comment. Gray's eyes softened with a smile, but the rest of his expression was somber. "Two. I've been trying not to frighten you off with my 'freakish intensity,' as I've heard some people call it. I purposely avoided too much talk of the future and focused on enjoying—immensely enjoying—the here and now."

Mia's breathing came easier. "I've been immensely enjoying it too."

"You don't know how happy that makes me." Gray took her hand and his thumb rubbed a circle on her wrist. "Three. I was going to wait until tomorrow to give you the heads up, but since it's almost time for you to rehearse, I'll tell you now. Check the Secret Keeper when you have a minute. It may or may not hold a valentine. Then, if you still have any worries at all about my feelings, let me know."

"What? But I won't be able to go until tomorrow. You can't seriously keep me in that kind of suspense!" Mia smacked him lightly with her free hand. He caught that wrist too and bit it gently. Then, growling like a maniac, he proceeded to kiss along the tender part of her inner arm. The sensation—even of this silly, jokey action—was alarmingly arousing and almost made her lose her train of thought. *Almost*. "Seriously, Gray, you have to tell me."

He lifted his mouth from her skin just long enough to mimic her teasingly, "Seriously, *Mia*, no I don't."

"It's not fair to torture me like this!"

Gray laughed wolfishly. "I could say the same thing about you. Besides you don't really want to ruin the surprise, do you?"

"I guess not," Mia grumbled, but couldn't help smiling at Gray's smug look. "Do you want to come to rehearsal with me?"

"No, sorry . . . I've got a bunch of work that needs done and I don't want you to feel like I'm here waiting for you. Have fun and I'll see you tonight. I'll carpool in with Jo and Callum."

"Argh," Mia exclaimed. "I can't believe you told me there's something in the tree when I can't go get it right away."

Gray grinned. "I confess I might've hoped you'd feel a bit of suspense, yes."

MIA HAD BEEN WILDLY ENJOYING the set. Good, and lame, music originated in every decade, but there was something about 80s tunes she found extra full of life and change, though maybe that was her age showing. As an extra bonus, with no shortage of melodrama, they made for fun performing. The crowd danced like crazy and there was barely swaying room on the floor when she and the band crooned yet another famous hair metal love ballad.

Gray was sitting by himself at a small table for two, nursing a pint and drumming his fingers in rhythm to the music. Every time Mia glanced his way, his eyes met hers—and every time it was like a physical touch that sent a warm current buzzing through her. She was burning with curiosity about the Secret Keeper's valentine, but hadn't been able to hound him further or beg for hints because they hadn't talked privately since he'd told her about it.

Now, however, on the second to last song she'd be singing, Mia realized something that she should've noticed earlier and it started to melt her happiness. Despite the cheery cacophony of music, voices and laughter and the jostling, dancing people, Gray only had eyes for her. If someone stopped and chatted with him, he nodded pleasantly and replied—but he never gestured for anyone to join him. She was sure Sam, Jo and Callum had each asked him to sit with them, but that he had declined. She was equally sure he'd been asked to dance by two different women—and had turned down those offers too. Even his two-seat table in the crowded pub seemed set apart.

Because Gray was smiling and having a beer and seemed into the music, she'd thought he was enjoying himself. Now the truth of the situation hit her. He was only there because she was. Because he was lovely and sweet, he was patient about the forced captivity, willing to endure it with a grin, exactly the same way Wolf resignedly lounged on his belly waiting for Gray to finish whatever business he had before he could return to where he belonged. The wild. Was she selfish to ask Gray to build a life with her outside the woods?

The song finished to enthusiastic, alcohol fueled applause, but Mia barely heard it. She gave a humorous, hand twirling bow when the band thanked her for joining them and told them—and the crowd—that the pleasure was all hers. There was more applause, then a DJ jumped in, so the band could have a break before their final set. Mia hopped off the stage and crossed the crowded floor in search of Gray. She was stopped here and there by people thanking her and telling her how great the band was and what a good time they were having. Everything about the event and its people felt better than the huge venues she used to play, but her heart was heavy all the same.

And then she was at Gray's table. He stood up with a wide smile as she approached. "Well, well, if it isn't the fabulous Mia Clark."

Something in her face must've told him she didn't want to be teased right now because his tone changed immediately. "You were—you are—amazing, Mia."

Mia smiled but hot saline burned at the back of her eyes.

Gray's smile lines transformed into furrows of concern. "What's wrong?"

She tried to speak but found she couldn't. She took his hand and jerked her chin slightly, motioning toward the door. He nodded and, still holding her hand, took charge of leading them through the boisterous crowd, politely but firmly forging a path.

Outside, the night air was cold and damp—a refreshing kiss on her skin after the muggy heat from the crush of bodies inside.

"Mia, what is it?" The concern in Gray's voice was palpable.

There was an old hitching post near the front of the pub, slightly away from the small group of smokers that crowded the entrance. Mia hefted herself up on it and Gray leaned into the V of her legs, then touched her chin and lifted her face a little. As usual his nearness was distracting and for a moment, lust warred with her sadness.

"Mia," he repeated. "What is it?"

She sighed and figured it was better to spill it. Just rip off the Band-Aid, so to speak. The pub's hum of conversing voices, background music and laughter reached into the darkness around them, and Mia motioned toward it.

"Are you having fun? Really?"

Gray's forehead wrinkled. "Yes, *really*. Why?"

Mia shook her head. "Because I think I need this. I can't just hole up in the woods like a hermit, or not forever anyway. I want that too, I mean I want *you,* but I need . . . other things as well. Other people, music, singing . . . a life of many parts."

Gray tilted his head and for a crazy second Mia half expected his tongue to loll like Wolf's did when he grinned. "And?"

"And you, like you said in your own words, are like Wolf. *You're* a lone wolf." Mia spoke in a rush, forcing herself to unload her concerns before she came to her senses and held them back in the desperate hope that she was wrong, that she and Gray could actually work.

Gray's mouth opened, but she motioned him quiet. "You only came tonight because of me. If I hadn't been singing with the band, you wouldn't have—not in a million years. And you're so great that for my sake, you actually appeared to not totally hate it. I almost fell for it, but then I realized," Mia shook her head to emphasize her words, "you're just being Wolf. Patiently waiting until I let you return to the wild where you belong. You wouldn't be happy living in town. I know it. And I wouldn't be happy, not long term, living so far away from everything, month after month, or I don't think I would—" She broke off, conscious that Gray had stepped back from her—just a little, but still.

She dropped her gaze, so sad and so sure she was spelling out the ending for them that she couldn't look at him as she finished. "I do want you, Gray, more than anything. And I do love you—more than I imagined loving anyone, ever, but we have an insurmountable problem." Mia took a deep breath and Gray waited. "Deep down, I'm not a wolf and I don't know where that leaves us, or how or if we go on from here."

Gray didn't say a word or make even the smallest sound in reply. And that wasn't her imagination. He moved even further away, till he was no longer framed by her legs, no longer within reaching distance. She pressed her hands to her scalding face. What an idiot she was! Why hadn't she kept her worries to herself, waited to see what unfolded over time?

A wheezing sound grabbed her ears and pulled her away from her self-flagellation. She looked up, appalled. Gray was hunched over and his shoulders were shaking. Was he ... crying? Had she hurt him that much? She wanted to die of regret—but wait. The noise didn't really suggest crying, so much as ...

Her dismay spiked to an all new level. He wasn't crying. He was laughing. Laughing while she was almost as sad as she'd ever been in her life? What the—

"Mia," Gray muttered, hands on his ribs. "You have to stop. You're killing me."

Fresh tears pricked her eyes. What about her sadness, about them not being together, was so uproariously funny?

Gray moved close again, still sounding strangled by mirth. "There is no 'insurmountable problem.' Of course you're not a wolf. You're a mermaid."

Mia's emotions were reeling and she couldn't utter a verbal response—but her heartbeat quickened with something like hope. Man, she never learned, did she?

He lifted her chin again. "I'm sorry for laughing. I was, I am, just so relieved."

She shook her head. "I don't get it. Why would any of what I said make you *relieved*?"

He tried unsuccessfully to hold back another laugh. "I guess I need to spell it out for you. I'm not *actually* a wolf. It's a figure of speech."

"Obviously, but—"

"No buts. I was only trying to say how loyal and attached I felt to you, not to suggest I'm some unhousebroken mongrel."

"I don't think Wolf would appreciate that description."

"I don't think Wolf would give two hoots about any human words I use to describe him." Gray's voice lost its teasing, amused note. "Look, Mia. I get why you're worried. It's even kind of sweet—except that I don't want you to think choosing to be with me means settling for some damaged half-life."

"But—"

"Let me finish," Gray whispered.

She nodded and bit her lip to keep from interrupting again.

"To be clear," he continued. "I don't think there's anything wrong with living away from the rest of society and being independent. I think it's got a lot going for it actually, but I also know there's value in having community—and I've always known that was your goal in coming here: to get to a place where you could stop living like a shut-in. Plus, you're a musician, a singer, a performer . . . *Of course* you need people."

Gray extended his palms to her in a slow-motion double high five. Cautiously, then with exuberance, she met his hands with hers. Their fingers knit together. "I'm sorry to be so nuts," Mia said. "It's just that one minute I feel . . . better . . . or at least healed enough that I'm ready for the future and whatever it holds—hopefully you. But the next I feel like some damaged reject, who may or may not be up to the challenges and risks of love. I'm always sure that whatever I'm feeling can't be trusted, that it's too good to be true."

Gray moved their clasped hands to his mouth and kissed Mia's knuckles. "That's how I feel too," he said slowly and seriously. "But maybe all people do, to some degree."

He has a point, Mia thought. There is no magical place of all-knowing wisdom or confidence. All you can do is the best you can with the information and experiences you've been given to date.

Gray's grip on her hands tightened and he had to clear his throat before speaking again. "When I said I want to be with you forever, I knew—and know—what that means and what I'll be giving up. Trust me, it's nothing compared to what I'll gain. We'll figure out where we'll live when the time arrives for us to do so—actually, you know what? Screw it."

"What do you mean screw it?" she asked, genuinely confused.

He released her hands and reached into his jacket and withdrew a thick envelope from its inside pocket. "I grabbed this from the Secret Keeper before I came tonight because I changed my mind, wanted to give it to you in person. I was going to wait until after we got home, but the time seems right."

He shifted his body so the beam from a nearby streetlight fell full on the notepaper she removed from the envelope. "But how—"

"No more buts. Read."

She flattened the creamy paper against her thigh and did just that.

Dear Mia,

It's still hard for me to believe that something good could come from such a near tragedy, but part of me wonders if you hadn't fallen in the river, whether I ever would've gotten up the courage to tell you how I felt. I worry that I might've continued on like the proud coward I too often show myself to be.

But you did have that close call. It scared the hell out of me, but it also forced me to admit something I would've violently denied, previously. There is something worse than having those you love stolen from you; losing someone you love when you don't have to. The idea that I would be so stupid, so shortsighted, so willfully blind that I almost brought that down on myself shames me more than you can know.

The past weeks have not just been the happiest of my life since before Celine and Simon were torn from me. They have been wonderful completely in their own right.

I have been trying to follow your lead, not wanting to pressure you with talk of the future or my desire that we spend it together because I know (or suspect) it will seem sudden. But I'm not, in case you haven't figured it out by now, very good at being casual. "Intense" is sort of my natural default, even when I try hard to override it.

Anyway, I don't need time. I have had nothing but time for years and I know my mind. My heart. I would like to marry you. I *want to be your husband, for better or for worse, in sickness and in health and all of that. Some people feel marriage is old-fashioned, even archaic, but I confess I don't understand how pledging to love and honor another could ever be anything but a good thing. So yes, call me old-fashioned . . . even I see the description fits me to a T. And I don't apologize for it. (Both of which probably come as huge surprises to you.)*

Gray had drawn two smiley faces beside his last line and she looked over at him, flooded with fondness. The cartoon grins were such a perfect show and tell of the whimsical, silly side of Gray that softened and balanced his deeply sober, serious side. He met her eyes, his creasing in amusement too, then nodded for her to finish the letter, as if knowing she hadn't read to the end.

Mia whispered the remainder of the letter aloud, as if doing so would help convince her she wasn't merely having a lovely dream. She really was seeing the words she thought she was.

I understand if talking about something as huge as marriage or forever feels too soon, so don't worry. I won't harangue you. Just let me know when and if you ever feel the same.

And in the meantime, I hope you'll accept

this small gift as a token of how I feel about you. It's something I made this winter out of an antique silver spoon. I thought I was merely seeking to fill the long, dark winter hours, but have since realized I had been fooling myself again. It was always meant for you, the same way my heart has been ever since I stumbled upon you mermaiding about in the lake.

Happy Valentine's Day, my love. May it be the first of countless many.

- G

Mia's gaze shot up to Gray's again. He nodded shyly and placed something on her palm: a thick, softly gleaming silver ring. She held it, speechless. Warmed by her body's heat and so perfectly polished it was soft to the touch, the ring was almost indistinguishable from her flesh when she finally slid it on her finger.

It was such a simple thing and crafted from such a commonplace item that if you'd told her ahead of time how beautiful the end result would be, Mia wasn't sure she would've believed it, yet there was no denying it. Beautiful it was.

"Have I allayed your concerns and fears?" he asked softly, resting his forehead against hers.

"And then some," she breathed, illogically close to tears. They were on the same page. They both saw their future unfolding *together.*

Gray leaned into her, the full weight of him heavy

against her core. "Good, then it's settled. All the other stuff's just details. We'll figure it out."

"But—"

"Oh come on, woman, throw your poor dog a bone and just give me a kiss. I've been watching you all night, unable to touch you. It was torture."

Mia closed her legs around Gray's muscular torso and felt him stiffen with pleasure and surprise. "Now that's what I'm talking about," he growled with a low, sexy chuckle. Then—making her wonder suddenly just how much beer he'd nursed—he raised his face to the sky and let out a wild howl.

The soft mumble of voices from smokers by the door went silent—then there was a burst of appreciative laughter and two male voices yipped and howled in reply.

"You're crazy," Mia whispered.

"I am," Gray affirmed and pressed his lips to hers. He kissed her hungrily and hard, taking her mouth with none of his usual gentle, letting-her-warm-up-to-it quality—and Mia was shocked by the hot, instant response that rocketed through her, despite the layers of civilization—and clothing—between them. A final, needed bit of self-knowledge lit up deep within her. She might be a mermaid, absolutely. But she had some wolf in her too. Maybe everyone did.

Epilogue

WOLF HUFFED AND GRUNTED SOMEWHERE in the bush nearby as Gray steadily moved along the once faint, now well-defined trail. He eased through an archway formed by two cottonwood trees that had grown close together over the years. The small lake, *their lake*, as he liked to call it, sparkled and flashed in the late evening sun. Rounding a stand of skinny jack pines, he paused to take in the view, and a rush of heat and pleasure ran to his face . . . and other parts.

There was a mermaid waiting for him. The fact that he'd already known she'd be there didn't keep it from being a happy surprise—just like every time he saw her. He hadn't gotten used to it, hadn't stopped thanking his lucky stars every day. She was beautiful from every angle, including the glorious back view he currently had. Her hair was coiled in a messy bun on top of her head, providing an unhampered view of creamy shoulders and a smooth back that curved into generous hips and a well-rounded—

Wolf chose that moment, of course, to scramble from the tree line and race along the rocky beach toward the narrow strip of sand separating land from water.

Mia heard Wolf's very unsubtle approach and turned. Wet and gleaming, she beamed at them both, giving Gray a breathtaking frontal view of the huge belly he'd been admiring the sides of seconds earlier.

As if reading his thoughts, Mia's hands went to the heavy swell of her lower abdomen and rested there, cradling its contents.

"This. Is. Heaven," she called. "It's the only part of the day I don't feel like I weigh eight hundred pounds."

Gray laughed, but stayed where he was, enjoying watching her—but knowing that before long, he'd have to take full advantage of what he still couldn't believe was his privilege: to touch, to take—

"Getting a good enough eyeful?" she called.

He shrugged.

Her stomach was as firm and full as the moon that had, hours earlier, risen high and joined the sun in the summer sky—fertile, his ever-smitten brain whispered. Lush. Mine.

Above her stomach, her small breasts were heavy and ripe, with dark, perfect nipples standing pertly from the water's kiss. Every remembered nuance of her body was so familiar and textured, it was like he was already touching her. Like he never stopped.

His body stirred and his face warmed. Was he the only husband who still stared at his wife this way, even though they'd been together for three years already? Even though she was pregnant—or especially so? He couldn't imagine ever tiring of her—and how he hoped she never tired of him. There was a bundle of clothes near his feet. He stooped, grabbed her towel, and held it out.

She shook her head and splashed in his general direction. "What's good for the goose is good for the gander. Get your ass in here."

He didn't need further encouragement. He dropped his jeans, stripped off his T-shirt and jockeys, and waded into the lake.

"So it's official. I'm on mat leave," she said as he got close.

He smoothed his arms around her slippery, slightly cold belly from behind and pressed his chin to her shoulder. "And how are you feeling about that?"

"Great, actually. Aimee will do marvelously with the store. I'm so glad I hired her way back when—and my students seem happy enough for a break in lessons. I'll probably lose a few, but that's life."

Her skin glimmered with beads of lake water. He pressed a kiss to the ridge of her clavicle.

"You're not even listening, are you?"

"I am *totally* listening," he said seriously. "I'm just also doing some other things at the same time."

She shrieked as he gently forced her legs apart and cold water found warm spots.

"Not here, not in the lake—not at this stage," she

panted.

"I know," he murmured. "I know. I'm just playing."

"Just torturing, more like it," she said with a soft groan, sliding against his hand.

"If it's any consolation it's hard on me too."

She grinned. "Yeah, I can tell. Very hard from the feel of it."

It was his turn to groan, half with humor at the terrible pun, half in frustration at what he'd started but wouldn't get to finish . . . yet.

"How about we move this party to the beach? I think it's time to stop playing and get to work."

"Get to work, hey?" she said. "Very flattering."

He laughed—then sighed when she shook her head. "Not yet. I want to cool off some more." She dove beneath the surface on her last word and he followed her.

"Would you ever have guessed this?" she asked when they came up for air.

"This?"

"You know. That first time you caught me here . . . that it would lead to this. To us. To summer months out here in paradise and the rest of the year on a small farm, all as . . . a family?"

Treading water, Gray undid her bun so that it trailed down her back in wet tendrils. "I couldn't have even hoped," he said truthfully.

Mia lifted her legs and floated on her back. When

she drifted near him, she caught his hands and placed them on her stomach. "I was thinking," she said softly, "that maybe, if our baby is a girl . . . she could be a Celine. Or if he's a little boy . . . a Simon."

A tidal wave of feeling nearly drowned Gray. How kind she was. How generous. For a moment he forgot to kick and sank a little in the water. He recovered quickly.

"No," he said firmly. "Our baby needs his or her own name. I'll tell them all about their brother, but I never want them to feel even the tiniest, niggling worry that they were some sort of stand in or replacement for Simon."

Mia looked thoughtful, still afloat and drifting. They were in shallower waters again though. Gray could just touch. He took her wrist, anchoring her. "Just like you are fully, in every way, *not* a consolation wife or a substitute for something I lost."

Mia's head bobbed and she darted a look at him, slightly surprised.

"I'm serious, Mia. I don't tell you enough. I'll never pretend to understand what happened to Celine and Simon, let alone be grateful for it—but I will always be awed that somehow you came to me, found me, took me on. You are the love of my life."

"The love of your life now," she whispered.

"The only love of the only life I have," he corrected. "The Gray who lived and loved Celine and Simon died when they did. This Gray you resurrected is all yours."

Mia smiled up at the limitless reaches of the sky. "I'll take it."

"Oh, you will, hey? That's good because you made your bed. Now you'll have to lie in it." Gray grabbed one of her ankles and tugged her down.

She shrieked and thrashed, splashing with abandon. He caught her wrists, pulled her slippery body against his, and kissed her until they were both breathless.

"I love you, Gray," she whispered happily as they half swam, half floated, arms and legs wrapped around each other.

"I love you too, mermaid," he said against her mouth. "And I hope it works for you that wolves mate for life."

Mia blinked away what Gray thought might be tears—but then decided must've been lake water because her smile was big and bright and lovely. "It works very well for me. Very, very well, in fact."

Gray's mind flashed on the memorial stone he'd finally had made for his beloved Celine and little Simon. Then his eyes rested on his precious wife floating in their serene wild place with her life-filled belly. He felt very full. Very fortunate.

There was so much hard stuff in the world, so much pain, so many unanswerable questions, but there was also so much beauty, so much good. And sometimes, when you were very blessed, there was even joy.

Dear Reader,

I hope *Reeling* had you reeling—and that you love Mia and Gray (and Wolf!) as much as I do. If my River's Sigh B & B series is new to you, you'll be happy to know you can "book" other romantic getaways in *Wedding Bands*, *Hooked*, *Spoons*, *Hook, Line & Sinker*, *One to Keep*, and *Silver Bells*.

Want to connect? Yay! Please visit www.evbishop.com, where you can sign up for my newsletter, and/or find me on Facebook, follow my Twitter feed (Ev_Bishop), or drop me a line at evbishop@evbishop.com. I'd love to hear from you! And on a similar note, reviews really help authors. If you'd be so kind as to leave a few words on Amazon, Good-Reads, your blog, Facebook, or anywhere else you hang out when your nose isn't in a book, I'd be very grateful.

Thank you so much for reading!

Wishing you love, laughter and adventure—inside the pages and out,

☺ Ev

Ev Bishop

About the Author

 **Ev Bishop** is an award-winning author, who lives and writes in a remote small town in wildly beautiful British Columbia, Canada, a place that inspires the setting for her cozy romance series, River's Sigh B & B.

She currently has eight novels published through Winding Path Books: *Bigger Things*, a standalone Women's Fiction title, and her River's Sigh B & B series, which consists (so far) of *Wedding Bands, Hooked*, *Spoons, Hook, Line & Sinker*, *Silver Bells*, *One to Keep*, and *Reeling.*

Ev also writes under the pen name Toni Sheridan (*The Present* and *Drummer Boy*, White Rose Publishing).

In addition to writing novels, Ev is a long-time newspaper columnist with the *Terrace Standard* and a prolific scribbler of articles, essays, short stories and poems.

www.ingramcontent.com/pod-product-compliance
Lightning Source LLC
Chambersburg PA
CBHW060405180626
46817CB00007B/2518